Sisters
of
Isis

2

Divine One

LYNNE EWING

HYPERION/NEW YORK

Published by Hyperion Books for Children, an imprint of
Disney Book Group. No part of this book may be reproduced or
transmitted in any form or by any means, electronic or mechanical, including photocopying, recording, or by any information
or storage retrieval system, without written permission from the
publisher. For information, please address Hyperion Books for
Children, 114 Fifth Avenue, New York, New York 10011-5690.

Printed in the United States of America
First Edition
1 3 5 7 9 10 8 6 4 2
This book is set in 12-point Griffo Classico.
Reinforced binding
Library of Congress Cataloging-in-Publication Data on file
ISBN-13: 978-1-4231-0343-1
ISBN-10: 1-4231-0343-2

www.hyperionteens.com

For Patty Copeland, my best friend forever, and her wonderful husband, my big brother Tom.

CHAPTER 1

The storm was worse than any Meri had seen since she and her mother had moved into the old Victorian house in Washington, D.C. Lightning blazed across the night, and within three seconds, thunder exploded. A short burst of hail hammered the windows, then stopped, leaving only the patter of rain on the glass. Meri couldn't rid herself of the strange and frightening feeling that the storm was somehow directed at her, a prophetic sign of bad days ahead.

A sharp hiss made her look down as lightning flashed again, illuminating her bedroom with shuddering light. A dark form crept across the carpet, tail flexing back and forth.

"Don't be afraid, Miwsher," she said as thunder rattled the walls. She assumed that the storm had frightened her normally bold cat.

She tossed back her covers and jumped out of bed, but as she started to run after Miwsher, her foot landed in something wet. She paused and swept her toes across a soggy groove in the carpet, then looked up, expecting to see rain trickling from the ceiling; after all, the house had been built in 1840. She didn't see a leak, but she did see her cat, perched on top of the tall chest of drawers.

Meri spun around. If Miwsher was there, then what was the other creature?

The backyard bordered on Rock Creek Park, and although bears no longer roamed in the wilderness behind their house, raccoons and foxes did. Maybe a small animal had used Miwsher's cat door to come inside and escape the downpour.

Meri tiptoed after the fleeing shadow, imagining the poor stray shivering with fear—but she didn't follow too closely, in case the trespasser was a skunk.

As she neared the stairs, an unfamiliar musty odor filled the gloom. The scent reminded her of cucumbers and wet soil. Although it wasn't a bad smell, some deep instinctual pulse within her took over—she stepped more cautiously now, not understanding her fear.

The middle landing formed a balcony from which she could see down into the living room below. As she leaned over the banister, wind hit the tall windows behind her, and the sudden noise made her jump. Thin branches slapped the panes. The leafless twigs made odd ticking sounds, louder than the rain.

She eased down the remaining steps, clutching the handrail so tightly her fingers ached. When she reached the last stair, a metallic crash came from her mother's home office, startling her.

It wasn't unusual for her mother to work late. She was the senior senator from California and had made one run for her party's presidential nomination. Everyone said she'd succeed in the next election. That worried the opposition party, but it also worried Meri.

The last time her mother had been a candidate, Secret Service agents had gone everywhere with Meri, including the high school dances. Their constant chaperoning had inhibited her. She was fifteen and still hadn't kissed a guy; not even a tight-lipped peck like most girls got on a dare in sixth grade. How pathetic was that? Some of her friends back home were seriously discussing birth control. She could only imagine how unexciting her love life would be if her mother actually won the election.

Then a bigger worry took over. Eventually, the agents would discover Meri's secret, and as sworn law-enforcement officers, what would they do? Was magic against the law?

She already feared that photographers would take her picture when she was doing something freakish. At one time she'd had two bodyguards assigned to protect her from the paparazzi. But after she'd learned about her true identity, Meri knew she couldn't expose the two men to the dangers she had to face. It had been hard enough convincing her mother that she didn't need the two-man escort. She couldn't picture herself trying to convince the

Treasury Department that the protection of the Secret Service wasn't necessary.

Meri paused in the doorway to her mother's office expecting to see the four-footed intruder padding across the desk. The night-light cast a pallid glow over the bookshelves, but nothing looked disturbed. Meri entered the room, brushing her hand across the polished wood, then gazed out the window and surveyed the backyard. Wind had toppled the iron lawn furniture and pushed it against the stones in the rock garden. Maybe that explained the sound she had heard.

From the corner of her eye, she caught a shadow moving toward her. She whipped around and bumped into someone. Before she could scream, a hand covered her mouth, and she breathed in the almond fragrance of her mother's lotion.

"It's me." Her mother spoke into Meri's ear.

"Mom," Meri said, her heart still pounding from the impact. She started to flip on the overhead lights, but her mother stopped her.

"Someone's in the house," her mother whispered.

"It's only a stray, or maybe a skunk," Meri said. "I forgot to lock Miwsher's cat door."

"No animal could make the noise I'm talking about," her mother said. "I heard the side gate opening."

Twice when they were living in California, someone had bypassed the alarm system and broken into their home. Now Meri wondered why her mother was prowling around the house like a detective, instead of calling the police.

Before she could ask, lightning struck the oak tree in the backyard, splitting the trunk. The night glowed orange, pulsing with spectral brightness, before fading back to gloom. Thunder shook the house. The vibration rumbled up Meri's legs and through her body.

Outside, sparks sputtered and swarmed around the branches, igniting twigs. Small fires spit more embers into the wind as rain quenched the flames. After that, the security lights went out. Immediately, the alarm system began bleeping, signaling that it had switched to battery power. Then the sound died.

For the second time that night, Meri had

an eerie sense that the storm's fury was directed at her. Warmth left her as fear took over, and the strange internal cold made her shiver. She eased in front of her mother, trying to shield her from the swelling shadows.

"Why didn't the backup system work?" her mother asked. She grabbed Meri's hand and pulled her down the hallway and into the kitchen.

Moments later, a match flared. Her mother lit a candle and handed it to Meri, but as she started to light a second one, something banged against the back door.

Meri jumped, almost dropping the candle. Wax dripped onto the hardwood floor.

"Was that the wind?" her mother asked, whipping around.

The knocking came again, in a steady, loud beat.

"It's probably a neighbor," her mother said, heading for the door.

But Meri had something more deadly in mind. "Don't answer it." She grabbed her mother's sleeve, pulling her back. Meri feared the storm had brought more than thunder, lightning, and hail.

The pounding continued, more urgent than before.

"A power line could be down," her mother said. "Maybe they've come to warn us."

"Mom, please don't," Meri said. She couldn't tell her mother about the real dangers facing the nation. She imagined the look of surprise and disbelief in her mother's eyes if she did. She doubted her mother would believe her. No one would.

She tried to think of a way to begin, but before she could, her mother had turned the dead bolt and opened the door. She peered outside. The chain lock, still engaged, jangled loudly as wind shrieked into the room, whistling around Meri and making the copper pans hanging from an overhead rack clang against each other.

A shadowy form slipped between her mother's feet and wiggled outside. Her mother squealed and slammed the door.

In the stillness that followed, her mother turned and faced Meri.

"What kind of animal was that?" she asked breathlessly. "Did you see it?"

Meri shook her head. "I only saw a tail."

The knocking came again, and before Meri could stop her, her mother opened the door. This time she said something to the person on the other side. When she shut the door and turned back, her eyes looked different, widened with shock.

"Please go to your room," her mother said. Her smile might have convinced the American public that she was calm and in control, but Meri didn't buy it.

"Who's there?" Meri asked, disobeying her mother.

"We are not going to discuss this," her mother said. "You don't have a need to know."

Her mother was on the Senate Intelligence Committee and had been called away before in the middle of the night because of urgent matters involving national security, but Meri didn't think an envoy from the president or the secretary of state stood on the other side of the door. Neither office could have inspired the dread she saw in her mother's eyes.

"I think I better stay," Meri said, feeling a rising need to protect her mother.

"Please," her mother added with a strange desperation in her voice. "I must speak to this visitor alone."

Reluctantly, Meri left the kitchen, but in the hallway she paused and listened, hoping to find out more.

"I said, your room," her mother's voice came from the kitchen.

"All right," Meri answered, already forming another plan. If she sat by her window, she'd be able to see the visitor when the person left.

The candle fire spit fitfully as she raced up the stairs.

In her room, she blew out the flame. Then she sat on the tufted seat in the bay window and stared out at the dark, caressing the birthmark on her scalp, near her temple and beneath her hair. She had always thought the mark was no more than an oddly shaped mole, until she had met Abdel. After that, she knew it was the sacred eye of Horus. It stood for protection, healing, and perfection, but also identified her as a Descendant of the royal throne of Egypt.

She thought of Abdel again. Her stomach fluttered pleasantly whenever she pictured his face. A dreamy smile stretched her lips as she traced his name on the window with her finger, then encircled it in a looping heart. Too often she daydreamed of kissing him, hugging him, and more.

She sighed. He was probably annoyed with the way she stared at him and giggled when he spoke. Her crush was pointless, because they could never be together. After all, he was her mentor and guide; at least, he was supposed to train her in the old ways. So far, he hadn't taught her how to handle her powers, or speak an incantation correctly. She didn't understand his reluctance.

Sometimes she had a feeling that he couldn't stand to be around her, and that made her long for him even more. Maybe something was wrong with her, she thought. Love wasn't supposed to hurt, but she couldn't help the way she felt.

The night she'd met Abdel, he had told her that he belonged to a secret society called the Hour priests. Back in ancient times, the goddess Isis had given them the Book of Thoth and instructed them to watch the night skies. When the stars warned of danger, the priests were supposed to give the book to the pharaoh. Nowadays, the priests found the next Descendants and gave them the ancient papyri.

Meri had thought the story was interesting, but she hadn't understood why Abdel was telling it to her until he added that he had been sent to the United States to find her. She was descended from Horus, a divine pharaoh of ancient Egypt, Abdel told her, and like all Descendants before her, she was being called to stand against evil and protect the world. Only the divine heirs to the throne of Egypt had the power to use the magic in the Book of Thoth to stop the dark forces.

Meri hadn't believed him, of course; nor had Dalila and Sudi, the two girls who had been summoned with her.

Even after he had given her a papyrus from the Book of Thoth, she had laughed at the idea that she could be divine. But when she started to leave, Abdel had stopped her, his expression determined and grim. He had clasped his hands around her head and recited an incantation to awaken the soul of ancient Egypt that survived deep within her.

Now she repeated the words, loving the feel of them on her tongue, the sound they made as they met the air. "Sublime of magic, your heart is pure.

To you I send the power of the ages. Divine one, come into being."

That night, a powerful feeling, both frightening and euphoric, had vibrated through her, growing in intensity, until she had thrummed with strange energy, her nerves and muscles tingling. What would have happened if her two bodyguards had stopped Abdel, or even hurt him?

The sound of the back door opening and banging shut startled her and tore her from her thoughts. She leaned forward and pressed her forehead against the cold glass, trying to see the visitor.

Rain and gloomy shadows hid whoever walked beneath the trees, but like the pharaoh Horus, who could transform himself into a falcon, each Descendant had the ability to change into an animal. Meri could become a cat. She didn't have control over the power yet, but she recited the incantation anyway.

As the words formed in her mouth, an ache rushed through her. Her legs trembled, and she clasped the edge of the windowsill, focusing her thoughts on remaining a girl; she needed only the night vision of a cat.

Whiskers prickled and popped from her cheeks, but then her pupils enlarged, and what had been lost in the swirling darkness below her now became visible and distinct.

She gasped.

Abdel stood beneath the trees without an umbrella or a coat to protect him from the storm. He looked as if he had rushed out into the weather wearing only a T-shirt and jeans; she didn't understand what he was doing in her backyard.

He looked up, and she wondered if he had sensed her watching him.

She jumped away from the window and glanced across the room. Luminous yellow eyes stared back at her from the dark. Her heart stuttered until she realized she was gazing at her own cat eyes, reflected in her mirror.

Slowly, she calmed herself and crept back to the window. Rain spattered the glass, and cold seeped over the sill, curling around her, but the draft alone didn't make her shiver. There was no reason for Abdel to visit her mother, unless . . .

A dull ache throbbed inside her chest. Maybe her lovesickness annoyed Abdel so much that he had come to talk to her mother about her behavior.

She sat on the window seat, tears warm in her eyes. She couldn't help it if she was infatuated with Abdel. Besides, she didn't want to stop liking him. She loved the way he made her feel, all pleasant ache and butterflies. She didn't care that her obsession was wrong.

Abdel turned and walked away, rain pelting his back, and in that moment she remembered the desperation in her mother's voice, the fear on her face. Her mother had acted as if she knew the visitor, but where would she have met Abdel, and why would she be afraid of him?

CHAPTER 2

A loud, grating noise blasted the quiet and jolted Meri awake. The high-pitched buzzing made her cover her ears. She jumped out of bed and looked out her window. Workmen with chain saws were already cutting the fallen tree into logs. From the cast of sunlight, she knew it was late and wondered why her mother had let her sleep so long.

She hurried to her closet, kicked aside the stack of new shoes, then stopped and stared at the line of muted gray and navy blue clothes in her closet. Her mother had hired a stylist to change Meri's surf-rat look into preppy, college-bound freshness. Meri didn't feel like herself in the clothes that Roxanne had bought, and no way was Meri going to dress boring and safe.

Then with a shock, she realized that Roxanne had taken down the photos of Meri with her friends on the beach in Malibu and replaced them with lists of fashion dos and don'ts. Meri tore down the papers with the curlicue writing and crumpled them without reading what Roxanne expected from her.

Frustrated, she took off her pj's and began dressing for school.

On Saturday, Roxanne had made Meri take out her nose ring, and in rebellion Meri had hemmed the skirt of her school uniform. Without even looking in her mirror, she knew she had made it too short. The hemline barely reached midthigh. In the public school she had attended back in California, that length would have been fine, but at Entre Nous Academy, the shortness was going to cause a scandal. She'd probably be sent home again.

She grabbed the black-and-white oxfords and a pair of socks, then rushed back to her bed, wishing she could wear flip-flops and toe rings instead.

As she bent over to tie the shoestrings, a curious, meandering path on the carpet made her stop. She looked closer and traced her hand over a thin, opaque membrane that matted the fibers together.

A fine film came off on her fingers. The animal that had broken into the house must have left the trail, but other than a giant slug, she couldn't imagine what kind of creature could have done it. But she didn't have time to puzzle over it. She needed to question her mother about Abdel's visit.

She raced down the stairs and burst into the kitchen. Warm air rushed around her, bringing the smell of fresh coffee and baked cinnamon rolls.

Ten or more candle stubs lined the sink. She didn't understand why her mother had lit so many candles and burned them down to puddles of wax, unless she had stayed up all night.

A clatter made her turn. Georgie, their housekeeper, rolled a bucket and mop across the floor and stopped near the scattered leaves and tracked-in mud.

"I didn't do it," Meri said, answering Georgie's scowl. She hugged the thin old woman, who grumpily remained silent. Then Meri dashed into the morning room off the kitchen.

Her mother sat at the table, dressed in a black suit, watching news programs with the sound turned off on the six televisions in the built-in cabinet that covered the east wall. The remote controls lay on the white linen cloth in front of her.

Meri sensed her mother's tension and wondered what the commentators had said.

"Where is everyone?" Meri asked and sat down.

Normally, staffers crowded the breakfast table, taking notes and talking on phones. Most were interns eager to break into political life, but a few had been with her mother through her entire career.

"Good morning," her mother said, but her gaze never left the screens.

"I saw all those burned-down candles in the kitchen . . ." Meri began as she poured Froot Loops into a bowl. "Didn't you go back to bed?"

Something on one of the middle televisions

caught her mother's attention. She grabbed a remote and pointed it at the TV; a reporter's voice filled the room: "Was it stress or lack of self-control?"

Meri looked up, not even sure her mother had heard her question. The news clip showed her mother walking away, surrounded by aides. The voice-over reported on her sudden weight gain.

Her mother jabbed the remote, and silence filled the room again.

"I could be the first woman president of the United States," her mother said angrily, "and they're focusing on my weight. Didn't they even listen to my speech? I know the opposition party paid someone to point out the pounds I've put on."

"Of course they did," a male voice said. "What's wrong with being full bodied?"

Stanley Keene, a reporter from the *Washington Post*, sat in the rattan chair in the corner, away from the sunlight. His huge belly hung over his lap. He pushed a cinnamon roll into his mouth, then wiped his fingers on a napkin and left it crumpled on the wickerwork arm of the chair.

"You know Stanley," her mother said.

"Morning." He smiled cheerily and brushed crumbs from his mustache.

"Good morning," Meri answered, trying to sound polite, but she had never liked Stanley. Even so, she felt bad that she had interrupted his interview with her mother. The opposing political party had been attacking her mother in order to divert attention away from her criticism of the president's foreign policy. Stanley had probably been giving her mother the chance to explain her views.

"Maybe we should go to my office." Her mother picked up her cell phone without waiting for Stanley's reply and called her driver. She grabbed her briefcase and started for the door.

"Mom," Meri said, pushing back her chair. She couldn't let her mother leave without finding out what Abdel had said.

Meri ran in to the living room.

"Mom," she called again.

Her mother turned, a haggard look in her eyes, and placed a hand on Meri's shoulder.

"Why did Abdel visit you last night?" Meri asked. Now that she had asked the question, her chest tightened in anticipation of the answer.

"Abdel?" her mother said.

"The person who knocked on the door last night," Meri explained, with rising frustration. Why was her mother pretending she didn't know him?

"That was my assistant, delivering a copy of a new bill for my review," her mother said.

"You can tell me," Meri said, her heart pounding. She was shorter than her mother and stood on her toes so she could see into her mother's pale eyes. The color always surprised her, so different from her own. No one would have thought they were mother and daughter. Meri's hair was black and curled in tight ringlets, her skin dark. Her mother's translucent skin revealed the blue veins in her temples.

"You seemed afraid of him," Meri whispered.

"What?" Her mother gave her a questioning look. "You mean last night? The storm scared me. What other reason would I have to be afraid?"

"Have I been a nuisance?" Meri asked, certain her mother was hiding something. "Was Abdel complaining about me?"

"Sweetie, I don't know anyone named Abdel." Her mother opened the front door. "And if I did, I wouldn't keep the conversation from you."

Meri stepped back. Her mother was lying, but Meri didn't know why.

"We really have to go," her mother said and kissed Meri's cheek. She started down the walk as the black Lincoln Continental pulled up the front drive.

"What would Abdel have said?" Stanley asked.

Meri spun around. Stanley was staring at her. A thin smile stretched his lips, making his cheeks rounder. He didn't look away when she caught his gaze. Was he just studying her the way journalists sometimes did, hoping to find a new angle?

After all, her mom wasn't just a candidate for office. She was also a single parent. Magazines loved to run that story. Meri had been an orphan living on the streets of Cairo before her mother had adopted her and named her Meritaten, after the daughter of the pharaoh Akhenaton and his wife, the famous beauty Nefertiti.

"What is it?" Meri asked rudely. "Why are you staring at me?"

Stanley shook his head and pushed past her, following her mother to the car.

Meri was desperate to find out more. She hadn't given up. She sensed that her mother was keeping something from her, and she didn't think it had anything to do with national security.

She eased back inside, already feeling the tingling in her skin as her body anticipated the change. She grabbed her book bag, clutched it close to her chest, and stepped outside, then stole around the corner to the side of the house, where no one could see her. She placed her house key safely in her skirt pocket and faced the morning sun.

"Amun-Re, eldest of the gods in the eastern sky, mysterious power of wind," she whispered. "Make a path for me to change my earthly *khat* into that of your beloved daughter Bastet."

A gentle energy whirled around her, caressing her cheeks and throat and making the leaves tremble. The metamorphosis began.

In response, she said, "*Xu kua.* I am glorious. *User Kua.* I am mighty. *Neteri kua.* I am strong."

A smile crept across her face as her clothing and backpack disappeared. She raised her arms in a lazy stretch, her soul already the essence of cat, and let the sun's rays warm her.

A sleek black pelt covered her skin. The silken fur shimmered in the light. Then her eyesight changed, and the sunshine became blinding. She stepped into the shadows. Her vision grew more panoramic but remained hazy around the edges.

A sudden feeling of pain made her press her fingers against her chest as she shrank down to cat size. She meowed in triumph, enjoying her feline instincts, and sniffed the urine the tomcats had sprayed; it was like reading a gossip column. A toad jumped in front of her, and she had to concentrate to pull herself away from the temptation to spend the day chasing after it.

She rushed to the front yard, her ears erect and facing forward, trying to hear her mother and Stanley over the shrill noise of chain saws.

Stanley leaned on a walking stick that she hadn't noticed him using before.

"Look at the cute cat," her mother said as Meri approached, mewling.

Stanley's head snapped around.

"I hate cats," he said and stamped his foot on the brick walk.

The sound crashed through Meri. Of all her

senses as a cat, hearing was the sharpest. She jumped back, arched her back, and hissed.

"Why did you scare the little cat?" her mother asked Stanley in a scolding tone. "I can't believe you were so mean."

Stanley bared his teeth. For a moment, Meri thought he was going to snarl. Instead, he poked the tip of his walking stick under her belly and nudged her away.

"Stanley," her mother said. "You're going to hurt the little thing."

"Cats make me edgy," Stanley explained.

But immediately Meri realized she had another problem. She recognized the snake-scale pattern on his walking stick. That was her wand. The one Abdel had given to her. What was Stanley doing with it?

The wand had the power to ward off evil, and even though Abdel had not shown Meri how to use its magic, she couldn't let Stanley take it. She leaped and tried to dig her claws into the metal-covered stick. Her nails screeched over the stones embedded in the bronze.

Stanley swung the stick and flung her into the air.

Her mother screamed in disbelief.

Meri twisted and squirmed and landed on her paws. She crouched low to the ground, lashing her tail back and forth in anger, and watched her mother and Stanley continue down the walk.

At the car, Stanley placed his hand on her mother's shoulder. His presumptuous touch made her mother scowl, and he took his hand away.

"Once we're in the car, we won't be able to talk freely," he said. "I need your answer now."

"Then my answer is no," her mother said.

"You have to help me," Stanley continued. "You know what I can do if you refuse."

"When I feel doubt," her mother said, "my answer is always no." She had an intimidating frown, and she was focusing it on him. "And no matter what you may believe, you can't blackmail me into changing my mind."

"Don't give me your final say yet," he said, softening.

The driver came around the car and opened the door for Meri's mother. He wore dark glasses, and even though Meri couldn't see his eyes, she knew by the turn of his head that he was scanning the neighborhood for snipers. His dark suit jacket was buttoned, and he probably had a Secret Service badge hooked on his belt.

"The Cult of Anubis is just a silly fad," her mother said as she climbed into the sedan, "something from California that has become popular here. I could ruin my career by doing what you want."

Stanley crawled into the car, taking Meri's wand with him.

Meri was too stunned to chase after him and reclaim her wand. Instead, she wondered what Stanley had tried to force her mother to do.

Like her mother, most Washingtonians believed the cult was only a fad that had become popular with young people who wanted to enjoy the spa and get in touch with their inner selves. Most members were unaware that the cult was ancient and evil.

Only a few people knew its true history. Anubis had once been the most important Egyptian funerary god. Then his cult had been taken over by those devoted to Osiris. But some of the priests who had served Anubis hadn't wanted to lose their power, so they had used Anubis and the Book of Gates in unholy ways to call forth demons and resurrect the dead.

Now the priests who had once served Anubis worshipped the wicked god Seth and planned to return the universe to the chaos from which it came. The leaders had brought the cult to Washington, D.C., hoping to find the Descendants and destroy the bloodline of Horus before the Hour priests were even aware of their scheme.

Meri shuddered, imagining what would have happened to her if Abdel hadn't found her first.

But her thoughts quickly turned back to Stanley. He knew something about the cult, and it had to be important for him to risk blackmailing her mother. She wondered what he intended to do if her mother refused to help him.

CHAPTER 3

Meri needed to hurry on to school, but the inborn pattern of a cat was growing stronger than her desire to transform. She stretched and rolled, soothing herself with a throaty purr, then licked her paw and rubbed it behind her ear. Just as she decided to waste the day lolling in the sunshine, black clouds spread across the sky and hid the sun.

She scrambled across the street and raced toward school, hoping to get inside before the first raindrops fell. When she passed the National Geographic Building, her whiskers twitched. Other eyes were staring at her. She tilted her head. Pedestrians marched around her, feet clomping on the walk. A man almost stepped on her, but no one was watching her with ill intent.

Still, the feeling didn't go away. She jumped onto the stone wall.

Across the street, Michelle Conklin stood sentinel at the entrance to Entre Nous Academy, holding an oversize umbrella, oblivious of the students who had to duck around the huge black canopy.

She was staring at Meri.

Instinctively, Meri's lips curled back, and she hissed. When Meri had started school at the academy, she had wanted to be popular the way she had been back in California, but Michelle had seemed determined to make that impossible. She had spread lies and warned other students away from Meri.

A raindrop landed on Meri's nose. More hit her back. Her feline self curled inward, and Meri could feel the change begin. She dashed around the corner, to an open courtyard directly across the street from Entre Nous. Then she scuttled under the branches of a hedge and crept back until she was certain no one could see her, not even Michelle.

She relaxed, and sweet pain rippled down her spine and tail. Muscle spasms made her yowl. Her bones stretched, and paws turned back into fingers. She lay naked beneath the thick growth of shrubs.

"Darn," she whispered. Where were her clothes? Panic made her hold her breath and concentrate.

Seconds later, her clothes appeared, but not everything did. Her feet remained bare, and her backpack was missing.

Her belongings didn't always make the transformation with her. Dalila and Sudi didn't have this problem. They always changed back fully clothed, in whatever they had been wearing before the switch.

She got up on her knees, spread the branches, and peered out. No one was watching. She jumped from behind the thicket and cursed silently, then brushed the dirt and leaves from her skirt. Abdel had to teach her how to use her power before she ended up naked in a public place and got arrested.

Meri crossed the street, dodging around traffic and hating the grimy, wet sludge beneath her toes. She needed to get to her locker before the first bell and put on her gym shoes. She eased through the crowd near the door. Kids talked in different languages and laughed at jokes that Meri didn't understand.

It was not the first time she had wished she could attend Lincoln High with Sudi instead. Meri's life had been casual in California; she hadn't had to worry about how low to curtsy when she met P. Diddy in a celebrity club. But in D.C., knowing who stood where seemed important. Most of the students at Entre Nous had protocol officers to guide them, and those who didn't took classes on etiquette at George Washington University.

"Pardonnez-moi," Meri stammered as she tried to push around two guys speaking a mix of French and Arabic. *"Assalamu alaikum,"* she said in Arabic. "Hello" was the only word she knew.

When they didn't budge, she became frustrated. "Can you just move it?" she said in her plain California English. That worked. They turned and looked down at her, then stepped aside.

She could feel her blush growing. If her mother expected her to make friends with students whose parents could contribute to her campaign, she was going to be miserably disappointed. Meri's bad manners were probably going to cost her mother votes.

She started up the front steps, anxious to get inside and warm her feet. A black umbrella swung in front of her and barred her way.

"Where are your shoes?" Michelle asked, and lifted the umbrella back over her head.

Meri stiffened. She didn't need this encounter. She already had too much on her mind.

"Is that the California style?" Michelle went on loudly, and glanced around to see if other students were watching.

"Why would you think this is a style?" Meri asked. "And why do you even care?"

"Sorry, I forgot," Michelle said too sweetly. "Barefooted probably comes naturally to you. Weren't you a beggar on the streets of Cairo? I'm sure that's what I read."

Before Meri could answer, Scott pushed

through the students who were shaking out their umbrellas and crowding inside.

"Why are you standing in the rain?" he asked, his wet curly brown hair hanging in his eyes. He didn't wait for Meri to reply, but grabbed her hand and pulled her onto the porch under the overhang.

He still had a California tan, even though he had moved to D.C. to get away from drugs and a bad scene back in Los Angeles. He lived with his grandmother, a physics professor at Georgetown University. His parents had hoped the change in environment would keep him clean, but he ran into other problems in the nation's capital. Meri wondered what his parents would have done if they had known what had happened to him.

"I was just inviting Meri to my party," Michelle said pleasantly, as she squeezed onto the porch between them and pushed Meri into the crowd. "And I hope you'll come, too, Scott."

"Sheesh." Meri rolled her eyes. When Scott was around, Michelle acted as if Meri were her best friend.

Michelle handed her umbrella to Meri, then pulled two turquoise envelopes from her messenger bag. She gave one to Scott and the second to Meri.

Meri folded the oversize invitation and stuck it into her jacket pocket.

"You're having another party?" Scott flicked his finger against the card. "You just had an extravaganza that cost more than most people earn in a year."

"It's practice for what I'm going to do," Michelle said and brushed back her two-thousand-dollar blond extensions before continuing, "I'm going to run the coolest club in the world and let only celebrities in. I'll be more famous than my father."

Her dad had a celebrity-courting lifestyle, but he did it to make money; he was the best fundraiser in D.C.

"I thought you wanted to be a singer," Scott said and winked at Meri.

"I've outgrown that," Michelle said seriously. "I want to do something more."

"And I'm sure your club will make the world a better place for all of us to live in," Meri said sarcastically.

"Thanks," Michelle answered. "I never quite thought of it that way. Maybe I can make a difference."

Scott laughed. "Are you for real?"

"It's hard to believe one person can do so much," Michelle said, beaming as if he had complimented her. "My father always tells me I'm amazing." She took her umbrella from Meri and ran inside after Cecil, the son of the ambassador from Romania.

Scott rested his hand on Meri's shoulder. "With all the money she's spending on entertaining us, she could practically support a third-world nation."

"I know," Meri answered. "Thanks for rescuing me again."

"Why is Michelle always on you, anyway?" Scott asked.

"I'm friends with Sudi," Meri said, wiggling her toes to get rid of the numbness.

"I don't think that's the reason," Scott said thoughtfully. "I think Michelle is jealous of you."

"Me? Why would perfect Michelle be jealous of me?" Meri asked. "She has everything."

"She doesn't have photographers running after her," Scott said. "You do, and she'd do anything to get that kind of attention. But the biggest reason for her jealousy is me." He smiled broadly. "She thinks I like you." He slid his eyes sideways, and Meri followed his look.

Michelle stood on the other side of the window next to the door. She was talking to Cecil but her eyes were focused on Meri and Scott.

"I think she thinks we're more than friends," Scott said.

"I've told her a dozen times that we're not," Meri answered. "I can't believe she's jealous. She has a life that anyone would want."

"Except for you and me," Scott said. "All we want is to go home."

Meri nodded. They both missed California and felt out of place in D.C. "You're doing a better job of fitting in," Meri said.

"That's because all the girls are crushing on me," Scott teased. He stopped and nudged her. "Come on. Cheer up. My conceitedness alone should make you laugh."

"I'm trying," she said and smiled up at him.

Scott held the door for her, and she stepped inside. A blast of dry, furnace heat hit her.

"So, why haven't you called Sudi?" Meri asked. She had promised Sudi she'd find out how Scott felt about her. "I know you like her, so what's the problem?"

"Strange things happen when she's around," he said. "She's bad mojo."

He tore open the invitation that Michelle had given him and brushed a hand across his forehead.

"What?" Meri asked and grabbed his wrist. He looked wobbly enough to pass out.

"Michelle's parents rented The Jackal, that new teen club. I can't believe she's having a party there," he said.

"Does that place mean something to you?" Meri asked. She had reason to be nervous, but she didn't understand why Scott was.

"The jackal is a symbol of death, isn't it? They used to haunt graveyards and feed on corpses." He looked at Meri and added in a whisper, "Their howling scares me. It's called the death howl."

"Have you ever heard a jackal?" Meri asked, surprised.

"Yes," he answered. Then he blinked, as if an odd flash of memory had left him. "No," he corrected and laughed loudly, making fun of his lapse. "How could I know what a jackal sounds like? It must be the old burnout in me speaking. I wouldn't know a jackal if one came up and bit me."

Her stomach felt queasy. She was suddenly worried about her only friend at the academy. "You're not—?"

"I'm clean," he said solemnly. "I don't know why I said what I did."

But Meri suspected that she knew.

The bell rang, and Scott walked away from her, pushing through the throng of students.

Meri stood in the center of the hallway, letting kids jostle around her, and didn't even move when someone stepped on her toes.

The Cult of Anubis had kidnapped Scott and replaced his soul with a demon's spirit. Meri, along with Sudi and Dalila, had rescued him and exorcised the demon, but she wondered if they had been completely successful. Maybe some kind of demonic residue had been left behind—something that Scott wasn't aware of on a conscious level— that made him afraid to go to The Jackal, even if it was for a party.

CHAPTER 4

After school, Meri wandered through the Eastern Market as another storm ripped through D.C. She hadn't eaten since the night before, and her stomach grumbled noisily. She craved a bite of apple or a dried fig—anything!—but her money was in the book bag she'd lost when she'd changed into a cat.

When a vendor turned to pick up a crate of oranges, she stole four green grapes, popped them into her mouth and chomped down. The sour taste made her wince. She squinched up her face, and when she opened her eyes, the man was staring at her.

Sudden guilt replaced her hunger pains. The unripe fruit hadn't even been worth the theft, but she couldn't tell him that.

"I lost my money," she tried to explain.

Before he could scold her, thunder crashed, and its violent shock waves rolled through the block-long market hall.

The vendor made the sign of the cross and stared up at the ceiling, watching the light fixtures swing back and forth.

The butcher across the aisle stopped hanging sausages over a wire and stepped down from his ladder.

Even the two photographers who had been stalking Meri suddenly forgot their prey.

She heard the photographer she knew only as Thimble shout, "This weather's not natural. No storm systems are coming down from the Arctic, and nothing's coming up from the Gulf."

"It's the Pentagon," the butcher announced.

He waited until he had the attention of all the shoppers near his counter. "They've learned how to control the weather."

"Then I wish they'd do a better job of it," the fruit vendor challenged and started rearranging the grapes.

"Just ask her," Thimble pointed at Meri.

Everyone turned and looked in the direction of his accusing thumb.

"She's probably heard her mom talk about these storms," he continued.

Meri shook her head.

Tourists and shoppers wearing plastic head scarves stared at her. Their eyes widened, and smiles broke out across their faces as one by one they recognized Meri. Cell phones and cameras came out.

Meri wasn't sure if it was hunger or nerves that was making her feel so faint.

The crowd inched toward her. The people within it seemed suddenly forged together at the shoulders, their camera lenses like third eyes all focused on her.

Meri spun around and darted past the

shoppers behind her. Her soaked tennis shoes made a wet, sucking sound each time one of her feet came down. She was starting to panic, not sure where to go, when Sudi stepped through the door near the bakery and shook out her umbrella.

Meri slammed into her. "Let's get out of here," she said in a breathless voice that didn't even sound like her own.

Sudi looked up. "Why's everyone staring at you?"

"I stole a grape." Meri pressed her fingers over her eyes, trying to get rid of the weird, spinning sensation. "Can I borrow some money? I need to eat."

"Sure," Sudi said and held the door open for Meri. Then she looked back over her shoulder. "You must have done something more than steal a grape."

Meri dashed out into the rain and waited for Sudi to open the umbrella. They linked arms and hurried toward the corner. The rhythmic squish-squash of Meri's shoes made Sudi laugh.

"What happened to your oxfords?" Sudi

asked. "I thought that was the only kind of shoe you were allowed to wear at that snooty school of yours."

"I lost them, along with my books and homework," Meri said. "The day has been a wipeout."

A vendor in a kiosk held out a spoon with a sample of candied pecan. Meri gratefully took it and bit down, enjoying the sugar seeping over her tongue.

"Did you talk to Scott?" Sudi asked.

"Not yet," Meri lied. She wasn't going to tell Sudi what Scott had said, not until she was able to coax a better answer out of him, anyway.

"Why not?" Sudi sounded disappointed. "Didn't you see him at school today?"

But before Meri could think up another lie, lightning forked across the clouds, curling and scattering into a hundred jagged veins.

Sudi squealed, and within seconds, thunder crackled, shattering the air. Meri clutched Sudi's arm.

"Am I the only one who thinks this weather is creepy?" Sudi asked. "My dad said that meteorologists have called a special meeting to try to figure out what's going on. I hate it. It feels so—" She stopped.

"So directed at us?" Meri asked.

Sudi nodded. "You don't think that's weird?"

"I think that's why Abdel wants to see us," Meri said, and at the same time she prayed that she was wrong.

"Life was easier when all I had to worry about was finding a party," Sudi said with a sulky frown. "I remember when not being able to buy a new push-up bra was a major problem."

Sudi had a key pass to all the trendy teen clubs, and she knew how to sneak into any D.C. party, even the swanky embassy affairs. Her parents were both lawyers at a prestigious law firm and worked twelve-hour days, seven days a week, so Sudi had the freedom she needed to live the party life she loved.

Meri looked across the street.

Dalila waved and ran across the intersection without looking both ways or even checking the traffic signal. The wind lifted her umbrella high over her head, and she didn't notice the car that swerved around her, or the one that stopped just in time. She had lived a sheltered life. Her parents had been killed in a cave-in while excavating a tomb in the Valley of the Kings. Since that time, Dalila had been homeschooled by an overprotective uncle. She didn't know how to do simple things that Meri took for granted, and apparently crossing the street was one of them.

"Let's hurry inside," Dalila said, already opening the door.

The smells of coffee, chocolate, and freshly baked cakes drifted out into the cold air.

"I feel as if the weather is a bad omen for us," Dalila said and whipped a red scarf from her head.

When Meri had first met Dalila, she shaved her head to flaunt her royal birthmark, the *wedjat* eye, which was identical to the ones that Meri and Sudi had. But since learning that the cult wanted to destroy the bloodline of Horus, Dalila had let her hair grow back, and now glossy black strands covered her scalp in a tight pixie. She had known about her royal heritage, but she had been stunned to discover the real meaning of the birthmark. She had thought she was being groomed to marry a Middle Eastern prince.

They followed the hostess to a table near the plate-glass window. Meri sat with her back to the room and ordered German pancakes and cappuccino without looking at the menu.

"Abdel was standing in my backyard last night," Meri said, and then she leaned forward and told Sudi and Dalila everything that had happened the night before, leaving out any mention of her crush on Abdel.

"Why would Abdel need to see your mother?" Dalila wondered. "You have to ask him."

"I will," Meri said, and then she described her morning encounter with Stanley and how she had discovered that he had stolen her wand. "He gives me the creeps, the way he stares at me."

"Do you think he knew what the wand was?" Sudi asked.

"Maybe he just needed it for support," Dalila suggested. "You said he was a huge man. My uncle uses a cane sometimes, because his weight makes his knees hurt."

Meri shrugged. "I suppose, but I'm certain the wand was hidden in my closet. Why would he go snooping around in there?"

"I'll bet he's a pervert looking for underwear," Sudi put in.

"Yuck!" Meri squealed.

"But even if he did take the wand because he needed a crutch," Dalila added thoughtfully, "we'll still have to figure out a way to get it back."

Meri started to tell them that The Jackal had opened but before she could, Abdel joined them.

"Good morning," he said and sat down in the chair to Meri's left.

Meri's heart fluttered, and her cheeks grew warm. Seeing him in person was so different, and so much better, than daydreaming about him. He was always more handsome than she remembered. She loved his dark eyes and hair.

"What's wrong?" Sudi asked and shook Meri's shoulder.

"Nothing." Meri shrugged Sudi's hand away.

"You're blushing," Dalila said, reaching across the table. She placed her hand on Meri's forehead. "Are you feverish?"

Meri pulled back. "I told you I'm fine." She tried to sound lighthearted, and laughed to show them that her blush meant nothing, but the giggle came out as a honking snort. Before she could calm herself, Sudi spoke.

"Ask Abdel why he was standing in your backyard," Sudi urged.

Meri couldn't believe Sudi had just blurted that out.

The waitress set a plate filled with thin folded pancakes in front of Meri. She gazed down at her food, ashamed and bashful. Her hair swung forward, and a strand fell into the syrupy fruit. She grabbed it and licked off the syrup without thinking, then rolled her eyes in embarrassment. Why did she always act so ridiculous when Abdel was around?

"Go ahead and eat," Abdel said in a gentlemanly manner, as if he thought she was waiting until he had his meal before she started chowing down.

Even though Meri felt faint with hunger, she was suddenly too nervous to eat. Her stomach had curled into a tight ball, and she knew if she took a bite she'd vomit.

"Abdel, why did you go over to Meri's house last night?" Sudi asked when Meri didn't.

"I sensed that Meri was in terrible danger." He touched Meri's hand.

Meri's fingers twitched, and she wondered if he could sense how much she liked him.

"But why did you talk to my mom?" Meri asked. She looked into his brown eyes and wished she hadn't. Her strength left her, and she had to place her elbows on the table to keep from keeling over.

Too late, she realized that she had jerked her hand away from Abdel. Had he noticed? Would he think she had done that on purpose because she didn't want him to touch her? When really, she wished she could push her pancakes aside and kiss him.

"I didn't talk to your mother," he said after a long pause.

His lie snapped her out of her swoon. Her mother had lied to her about their meeting, and now Abdel had, too. What were they keeping from her?

"Someone knocked on the back door," she said, more frustrated than angry. "My mother invited the person inside. If it wasn't you, then who was it?"

"I saw your mother look out at the storm, but I never saw anyone standing on your back porch." He held up his palms, as if that would convince her that he was telling the truth. She had never noticed the scar on the pad of his thumb before. "Maybe a friend of your mother's came over before I arrived."

Meri thought of Stanley. Her mother would never have let an ugly old troll like Stanley spend the night. So who had she let in?

"An animal was loose in her house," Dalila added.

Abdel studied Meri with such an intense look that her swoon came back.

"Did you see what it was?" Abdel asked.

"I only saw its tail," Meri answered.

"Is it possible that what you saw was a snake?" Abdel leaned closer to her.

Meri had convinced herself that the dark form had only been the tail of a squirrel, or a stray cat, but she supposed the shadow wiggling up and down and side to side could have been a snake.

"Maybe," she answered, not liking the concerned look in his eyes.

"I think the creature was Apep," Abdel said, sitting up straight again in his chair.

Dalila dropped her fork. "The soul-hunter is here?" She pushed her plate away. "How could Apep escape from the Netherworld?"

"I believe the cult summoned him," Abdel answered.

"But when we saw Apep last, the snake was so large," Sudi argued, "he would have stretched from here to Capitol Hill, so how could he fit inside Meri's room?"

Meri shuddered, remembering the fine film she had found on her carpet that morning. In the Netherworld, the giant serpent had slithered toward them, leaving a frothy trail of green scum on either side of his body. An angry god had sent them to Apep, and Meri had hoped never to encounter the snake again.

Tears filled Meri's eyes as she realized the danger she had unknowingly brought into her home.

"Apep brings violent storms." Dalila crossed her arms over her chest, as if feeling a sudden chill. "And the weather forecasters have no explanation for the thunderstorms."

Dalila's uncle and guardian was the famous Egyptologist Anwar Serenptah. He had immersed Dalila in ancient Egyptian culture, magic, and religion, so she knew things that Meri and Sudi hadn't learned yet.

"But I don't understand how Apep was small enough to fit into Meri's room," Sudi said, voicing her concern again. "You could be mistaken, couldn't you? Maybe it was just a raccoon or a possum."

"It's not easy for something from the Netherworld to come here," Abdel explained. "The creature is weak and small at first, until it adjusts to our world."

"Then what?" Sudi asked.

"The three of you need to stop Apep before the demon becomes too strong," Abdel said and broke eye contact.

"But there's something you're not telling us," Dalila said.

"In the past, only the god Seth has been able to resist the serpent's stare," Abdel said.

"But we escaped Apep once already," Meri put in.

"Yes, you *escaped* the soul-hunter," Abdel

answered. "You weren't fighting Apep, or trying to defeat and vanquish the demon."

"He's right," Dalila agreed. "We only had to run from him."

"I'll study the Book of Thoth," Abdel said, standing abruptly. He looked down at Meri. "And until I find a protective spell, you must be cautious."

"You always have us search for the information ourselves," Dalila said. "Why is this time different?"

"We can't make a mistake this time, because . . ." Abdel seemed to be debating within himself whether or not he should tell them the truth.

"Tell us," Sudi pleaded. "It's always better to know."

"I'm certain Apep has been summoned to destroy the three of you," he said. "I think the creature stole into Meri's house, hoping to kill her in her sleep."

"Why didn't he?" Meri asked as a shiver crept up her spine. "Apep was under my bed."

"Perhaps the spells I cast stopped him," Abdel said, "or maybe Miwsher scared him away."

"That's why you were in my backyard?" Meri asked, feeling a burst of warm emotion. "To protect me?"

"Yes, divine one," he answered. "That is my duty."

Meri smiled, and he looked away from her.

"All three of you must give me your solemn promise that you won't do anything until we meet again," he said. "What I need to do may take some time, and I don't want you venturing out on your own, the way you did with the mummy."

"I promise," Meri said. So did Sudi and Dalila.

The girls had tried to deal with a mummy that had been summoned to destroy Sudi, but instead of getting rid of the creature with a simple spell, Sudi had placed a love spell on it and turned an uncomplicated problem into an impossible one.

Apparently satisfied, Abdel turned and left.

Meri watched him. She couldn't just let him leave. She jumped up.

"Where are you going?" Sudi asked.

"I forgot to tell Abdel that The Jackal had opened," she lied.

"I'm sure he knows," Dalila said. "You haven't eaten your pancakes."

"I'm not hungry," Meri answered over her shoulder.

She ran outside. Rain hit her in a solid sheet, soaking through her clothes. She splashed through the puddles, chasing after Abdel. She wanted to invite him to Michelle's party.

"Abdel!" She yelled and waved.

He turned and held out his umbrella, inviting her under its protection. She stepped next to him and he placed an arm around her.

"You're shivering," he said, pulling her close to him. "Your teeth are chattering. Didn't you bring a coat?"

"It's a long story," she said, cuddling against him.

Now that she stood close to him, pressed against his warm chest and looking up into his eyes, she felt too shy to ask him to go to the party with her. She hadn't thought this through.

"What did you want?" he asked when she didn't speak. "Is something wrong? Did something more happen last night?"

She shook her head. He leaned down, studying her eyes, his breath mingling with hers. She wondered if he could hear her galloping heartbeat over the rain.

"Meri," he said gently, "if nothing is wrong, I need to go home and study."

"I was wondering if you—" Her stomach growled noisily, and she pressed her hands against her waist, trying to stop the sound.

"Why didn't you eat?" He took her elbow and led her back to the café. "You need to finish your pancakes."

"No!" she said loudly.

"What is it?" he asked.

He looked like any sixteen-year-old guy, but if he was an Hour priest, then he had probably lived for a few thousand years. She wondered how many girlfriends he had had in that time. Probably none that looked like a wet surf rat, like Meri. She wished she could be glamorous like Dalila, or have Sudi's confidence. He'd probably never go out with a foolish, simple tomboy.

"Never mind," she said and started to walk away.

He kept pace with her, holding the umbrella over her head. "If something happened, you have to tell me," he said.

"Just go back to all your Cleopatras," Meri said glumly. "I imagine you'll be happier with them."

He chuckled. "How did we get from Apep to Cleopatra?" He stepped in front of Meri and made her stop. Then, with his free hand, he lifted her chin until she was forced to look into his eyes. "Tell me."

"I just wanted—" she stammered and stopped. She should never have followed him outside. She wasn't good at flirting.

Abdel frowned.

"Why do you always act like I'm a nuisance?" she asked. "I can't control the way I feel."

Understanding softened his eyes. "You don't need to feel afraid," he said. "I promise, I'll protect you. I'll find a way for you to stop Apep."

"That's not it." She looked down at a puddle, suddenly realizing that he wasn't going to leave until he knew what was bothering her. She took a deep breath and lifted her head.

"Michelle is—" she started again and stopped abruptly when he glanced at his watch. "Can't you see I'm trying to ask you out?" she asked, completely flustered.

He didn't say a word, and she couldn't read his expression. Then he smiled. Was he laughing at her?

"You're the most irritating person I've ever met in my life!" she yelled.

A sudden burst of light blinded her, and at first she thought it was lightning. But then another flash and another quickly followed the first. Thimble and his companion had jumped from an SUV parked at the curb and were taking photos of what they probably thought was a lovers' spat.

Meri turned and stomped away, her shoes making that terrible sucking sound. She couldn't even ask a guy for a date, let alone have a first kiss. Between the paparazzi, the Secret Service, and her own inability to deal with guys, she probably wasn't going to lose her virginity until she was forty-one, if then.

It felt like the worst day of her life.

The photographers kept walking with her,

jumping in front of her and taunting her, trying to trigger a reaction, but she was too sad to react. After the initial burst of anger, she had been left with a funny, hollow feeling inside. She was glad the rain was pelting her face so they couldn't see the tears welling up in her eyes.

When she didn't make faces at the camera, or try to run, the photographers became bored with her and left.

As their SUV drove away, she let the tears fall. Why had she moved here? She imagined her friends back in L.A., down at the beach. At least there, she had been able to lose herself in the waves.

She had been so deep in thought that she hadn't heard the voice calling her name.

When at last the shouting came into her awareness, she brushed back her dripping wet hair, wiped her nose, and turned with a huge smile on her face, expecting to see Abdel running after her.

CHAPTER 5 ~&

"Michelle's having another party," Sudi yelled, holding her umbrella over Meri's head.

Meri looked down the street. Abdel had vanished. She folded her arms over her chest against the cold. Her jacket was soaked and stank of wet wool, but worse, rain was dripping down her back, and her hunger was turning into sharp stomach pains.

"How did you find out?" Meri asked over the

sound of her teeth chattering. "I thought Michelle was only inviting kids from Entre Nous."

Sudi put her arm around Meri and squeezed her tightly, trying to make her warm.

"Carter got an invitation," Dalila explained. "But I don't have a cell phone—"

"So he called me because he knew Dalila was with us and he wanted to invite her," Sudi raced on excitedly, her happiness escalating to a level that Meri couldn't bear. "We have to go," she continued. "Scott will be there. Let me see the invitation."

When Meri didn't move fast enough, Sudi snatched the envelope from her jacket pocket and tore it open.

"Read the fine print," Meri warned. "It's going to be a karaoke party, and Michelle expects everyone to sing." Meri felt miserable, and it wasn't just from shivering and not eating. Without Abdel, the party sounded like a night in hell.

"Singing will just add to the fun." Sudi pulled out the invitation. "Besides, it can't be bad if Michelle is giving it. She spends like a zillion dollars on her gala fetes."

Sudi's excitement ended. A high whistle

escaped her lips. She handed the invitation to Dalila and shook her head.

Dalila began reading; her regal bearing seemed to slump. A sudden gust tore her umbrella from her hand, and she didn't even try to catch it. It cartwheeled down the street, a streak of red in the gray storm.

Dalila stared at Meri. Rainwater ran in tiny rivulets over her perfect features and twisted down her thin neck.

"We have to go." Dalila pointed to the location written on the invitation.

"Just because it's at The Jackal?" Meri didn't finish her sentence but turned and started tramping through the puddles. They couldn't make her go just because she was a Descendant.

Sudi ran after her. "Why are you so upset?"

"We don't have time for parties. We have to fight Apep. All right?" Meri answered, but that wasn't the reason for her anxiety. "I think that's enough to make me tense." She continued with her lie. "My life cannot get any—" She stopped. Every time she had said that lately, another problem had been dumped on top of the ones she already had.

"I'm going to talk to Abdel and see if he wants to go," Dalila said behind her.

Meri spun around. She hadn't sensed any teasing in Dalila's voice, whose expression remained tense.

"I think he should be with us the first time we go to The Jackal." Dalila handed the soggy invitation back to Meri. The blue ink had run until the letters were long blotches.

Meri let it fall to the ground, and the rainwater washed it into the gutter.

Then Dalila and Meri linked arms with Sudi and squeezed under her umbrella. They began walking toward the Capitol.

"Abdel won't go to a party," Sudi said. "He's way too stuffy. He probably doesn't even know how to dance."

Meri started to defend Abdel, but Dalila spoke first.

"Do you think this means that Michelle has joined the cult?" she asked.

"Michelle's too self-centered to join any group that doesn't center around her," Sudi answered bitterly.

But Meri wondered. Perhaps Michelle hated Meri for a reason other than simple jealousy. Maybe they were enemies fighting on different sides of the ancient battle between order and chaos.

CHAPTER 6

M eri stared into her dressing-table mirror and smoothed on lip plumper. She loved the sting, but when she puckered up, she didn't see any change. Then, she worried that the thick layer of balm might make her lips taste like Vicks. She grabbed a Kleenex and rubbed until her lips burned. When she had finished, tiny flecks of tissue covered her chin.

Dalila and Sudi stared at her.

"Why are you so nervous?" Dalila asked.

"I don't know why I care what I look like," Meri complained. "The cult is probably using Michelle's party to trap us, anyway." Meri threw down the tube and sprawled across her bed. "Forget it. I can't go."

"Of course you're going," Sudi said as she added lilac eye shadow above her own spiky lashes.

"I can feel magic gathering around us," Dalila said. She took a kohl liner from her velvet drawstring bag, kneeled beside the bed, and gently began outlining Meri's eyes.

"How do you always stay so calm?" Meri asked, loving the attention.

"I'll share one of my secrets with you sometime, when you really need it," Dalila said. "But if I showed you right now, you'd laugh at me."

"Try us." Sudi pulled a sheer top over her silky camisole. "Do you royals really have secrets that you keep from all the plebeians like me?"

"I have something better than a secret," Dalila said mysteriously. She stood and picked up her velvet bag, then carried it over to the bay window. She pulled out three red votive candles and set them on

{ 69 }

the sill. After that, she took out a book of matches. "Ancient Egyptians didn't have matches or use candles, but I needed one flame for each of us, and this was the best I could do."

"For what?" Meri asked, bouncing off the bed and joining her.

Dalila seemed breathless and excited. Her enthusiasm spread through the room, infecting Meri.

Sudi sat down on the window seat, still using a fluffy makeup brush to sweep bronze shimmer over her cheeks. "What are you doing?"

Dalila smiled. "Thoughts are like magnets, and we draw into our lives what we think about most."

Sudi and Meri nodded.

"This past week we've been focused on the cult and Apep," Dalila continued.

"What else should we be thinking about?" Sudi countered and tapped the makeup brush against her palm.

"This could be our last—" Meri stopped. She couldn't bring herself to say the word.

"But if it is our last night," Dalila went on, "then let's concentrate on something that will give us joy." The match flared, and she lit the candles one at a time. "Great Isis, goddess of love, hear us," Dalila began. "We entreat you to turn our thoughts to love and romance."

Meri smiled. Unexpected warmth flowed up her arm and into her heart. She touched her chest and suddenly imagined Abdel's lips touching hers. She caught her breath and placed her fingers over her mouth. The sensation felt too real.

"Woo-hoo!" Sudi shouted. "Did you put a spell on us?"

"No," Dalila said. "Isis made you stop worrying about all the bad things that could happen, and she turned your mind to concentrate instead on all the good fun you're going to have tonight."

"But you must have done something." Meri strode over to her full-length mirror. Dalila had made her eyes smoky and sexy. She suddenly felt all glamorous and seductive in her chiffon skirt and lace tunic. Her bare legs looked luxurious and long in her spiky sandals. She wiggled her toes to show off the three toe rings she wore for good luck.

"Wow," she whispered, then spun around. "Dalila, what did you do, really?"

"Nothing." Dalila smiled. "Isis banished your doubts so you could feel the confidence with which you were born. That's all."

"Come on, gorgeous," Sudi teased and grabbed Meri's arm. "Let's go, before all the cute guys are taken."

"You mean, before Michelle gets Scott," Meri teased back.

Sudi stared at herself in the mirror. "With the way Dalila made me look tonight, that's impossible."

"I told you. I didn't do anything," Dalila said lightheartedly. "You're just feeling what's inside you."

Meri set her cell phone on the dressing table and tucked her house key into her skirt pocket. She wanted her hands free—she smiled to herself, imagining Abdel—just in case the mental image she had had of the kiss came true.

CHAPTER 7

Less than an hour later, Meri, Dalila, and Sudi strode down Seventh Street in the Penn Quarter, their high-heeled sandals tapping out their pace. The spicy smells from the restaurants in Chinatown wafted around them as they neared The Jackal, and the pulse of music came through the walls, flowing out into the night.

"We're here to party," Sudi reminded the other two and gave them each a mint from her tin.

"Party," Meri agreed without any enthusiasm and bit into the candy.

"An arit sen tet er a," Dalila recited as they stepped past the gilded wooden figures of pharaohs that lined the façade.

"May they not do evil to me," Meri whispered, repeating Dalila's invocation in English. Sudi mouthed the words with her.

Meri pushed through the revolving door. The rubber edges of the black glass panels made soft, swooshing sounds as the door turned.

Once inside, they stood in an entrance hall paved with glittering gold tiles and flanked with statues of reclining black jackals. From hidden speakers, the wild dogs' howls filled the passageway.

"Do you think it's a trap?" Meri asked.

"There's only one way to find out." Dalila started forward with the confidence of a queen.

At the other end of the entry, two bare-chested men wearing low-slung white kilts opened a second set of doors and waited for the girls to step through the threshold into utter darkness.

"Jeez," Sudi muttered. "Where's the party?"

The doors slammed behind them, leaving them in complete blackness. They waited, clutching each other, as their eyes adjusted to the gloom.

A warm air current encircled them, caressing their arms and bringing the scent of sun-scorched sand.

"Are we sure we're inside the club?" Dalila moved away from them toward a glimmering light.

Meri joined her, spellbound. A starry night covered the huge, vaulted ceiling above them.

"It looks like we're standing near the pyramids on the Giza Plateau," Dalila said, staring at the scene of a desert night painted on the wall.

The angry thump of music broke their trance.

"Come on," Sudi yelled excitedly.

Meri ran down a curving ramp that led out on to a vast dance floor.

Light shuddered across the dancers, and the beat rushed through Meri with a hypnotic feel, enticing her to move.

The fragrances from designer perfumes filled the room, mixing into one blissful scent. She flung her hands over her head and slid between two guys. Sudi and Dalila moved with her, hips undulating, bodies close, pressed next to strangers on the crowded dance floor.

A guttural yell made them stop. They glanced at each other.

"Is someone hurt?" Dalila asked.

"That's someone's pathetic attempt at singing," Sudi explained.

Two voices squawked and bawled, destroying the guitar-driven music.

Meri and Dalila started laughing.

Sudi grabbed their arms. "Let's find out who's ruining the song."

Scott and his friend Carter stood onstage, singing off key and laughing at their inability to read the lyrics scrolling on the prompter.

"You guys need help!" Sudi's ex-boyfriend Brian yelled as he jumped up on the stage, joining them. He swung his head and began playing air guitar. Then he pushed between Carter and Scott, his lips on the mike. His deep, hoarse voice made everyone laugh.

Brian's new girlfriend, Dominique, placed her hand over her mouth and turned her back to the stage so he couldn't see her giggling.

"I love karaoke," Sudi said, beaming. "It's making Brian look like a fool."

Her breakup with Brian had been bad, but she had never told Meri everything that had happened between them.

"Get off it, Brian," someone yelled. "We want to dance, and you're killing the music."

Brian answered with an obscene gesture.

More kids booed him.

Sudi stopped laughing; her nervous stare made Meri take her hand.

"Are you all right?" Meri asked.

"Brian's getting upset," Sudi explained, no longer enjoying the taunts flung at him from the audience. She began easing back, pulling Dalila and Meri with her.

Without warning, Brian broke into a run, his footsteps pounding loudly. When he reached the edge of the stage, he dove onto the audience, his arms spread wide. Kids squealed and ducked. He landed on enough people to cushion his fall and cause pain for others.

Guys cursed and complained and dumped Brian in front of Sudi.

Brian and Sudi glared at each other; Brian's lip curled as if he were going to say something, but before he did, Dominique placed her arms around his waist and leaned against his back.

"You were marvelous," she said in her French accent.

Brian smiled broadly. "Yeah, marvelous."

Sudi rolled her eyes, but Brian didn't catch her look of disdain. Meri wondered what he would have done if he had.

Suddenly, Carter shoved through the crowd.

"I was afraid you weren't going to come to the party after all." He kissed Dalila's cheek. His lips lingered, and he whispered something into her ear.

Dalila placed her hands on his chest.

A slow song began, and Carter danced Dalila away from them.

"I hate that she's with Carter," Sudi said to Meri. "I tried to warn her."

Carter attended Lincoln High and was one of Sudi's best friends, in spite of his reputation as a heartbreaker.

"I know," Meri agreed, as a jealous ache filled her chest. "But it's not fair. Dalila has lived a sheltered life, and yet she's so natural with the guys."

"Maybe if you believed you were being reared to marry a king, a guy like Carter wouldn't be a challenge to you, either," Sudi offered and squeezed Meri. "Besides, all your fidgeting and giggles are adorable."

"I doubt that," Meri answered, trying to squelch her envy before it turned into bitterness.

"Let's go find the buffet," Sudi said. "Chocolate will make you feel better."

Meri started after her, but Michelle blocked their way. She had added lash extensions, and her skin had the glow of self-tanner.

"Meri, I'm so glad you brought friends," Michelle said, even though her heavily lashed eyes expressed anger. "Hi, Sudi," she added in a petulant tone as Scott pushed into their circle.

"Scott." Michelle posed seductively.

"Hi, Michelle," he said, and then, ignoring her, he turned to Sudi. "Do you want to dance? The singers aren't the best, but—"

"I wanted Sudi to sing," Michelle broke in. She pursed her lips in a babyish pout. "It's my party, and everyone has to perform."

"Sorry," Scott said, throwing Michelle a broad smile. "Sudi's taken."

Michelle watched Sudi and Scott until they disappeared behind other dancers. Then she wheeled around and scowled at Meri.

"Look at what you've done. Sudi's going to steal him from both of us. She's such a—" Michelle interrupted herself with a loud huff and ran her fingers over the hem of her ruffled pink mini. "I'd tell you what she is, but I don't use that kind of word, because it's too déclassé."

"She's really popular and well liked," Meri offered. "Is that what you were going to say? That she's such a great person?"

Michelle looked at Meri with the purest expression of hate. "Next time, don't bring any tag-alongs unless you get my approval first." She stomped off.

But something other than Michelle was bothering Meri. She squeezed into the crowd, unmindful of the feet stepping on her toes, and continued shoving through the throng of dancers until she could see Scott and Sudi again.

When she had talked to Scott about Sudi at

school, he had said that she brought him bad luck. But at the moment, he was holding her and looking into her eyes as if he were about to kiss her. That worried Meri, and she wondered what had changed his mind. She hoped it was how gorgeous Sudi looked that night and not the demon growing stronger inside him.

An odd tingling on the back of Meri's neck made her turn around.

A man Meri recognized as the club owner stood at the edge of the dance floor, staring angrily at her. His head was shaved, and his scalp reflected the dim light. He wore a tailored suit and a black sweater. A large gold ankh hung from his neck, a talisman that kept him alive. Meri had seen him perform arcane rites while dressed in leopard skins, his eyes lined in kohl; she had also watched him die, when Sudi tore the ankh from its chain. He was the high priest of the cult. They had encountered him when they had rescued Scott.

Dancers bumped in front of Meri, crowding between her and the club owner.

When finally she made her way to the other side of the couples, the man was gone. Now she wondered how many of the kids at Michelle's party had joined the cult. And if they had, she hoped they weren't dedicated to bringing chaos into the world.

Unexpectedly, someone grabbed her arms. She flinched and turned around, expecting to see the club owner. Instead, Jeff smiled down at her. He was a junior at Lincoln High, and a friend of Sudi's. She had introduced him to Meri at Michelle's last party.

"You look pretty." He slid his hands around her waist. "I was hoping you'd be here tonight so we could dance."

But the way he caressed her made her think he wanted to do more than dance. She tried to ease away and keep space between their bodies, but he pressed closer, his jeans rough against her thighs.

She pushed against his chest.

In response he smirked. His fingers slipped under her tunic, and he ran his palms over her bare skin.

She stiffened.

"Why are you so nervous?" he asked, grinning at her jumpiness. "I thought you liked me."

"As a friend." Meri tried to slip away from him.

He leaned down and nuzzled her neck.

"Jeff!" someone shouted.

Suddenly, Sudi was there, forcing herself between them, her hips slinking against Jeff, making him drop his hold on Meri.

"You promised you'd dance with me," Sudi said with a flirty smile and purposefully stretched her arms, letting her lacy top and camisole rise in a tease that gave Jeff a peek at her flat stomach and hip bones.

Scott stood nearby, watching Sudi. He placed a comforting arm around Meri and spoke into her ear. "Sudi said we had to rescue you," he said. "Was she right?"

"Yes." Meri let out a long sigh. From the corner of her eye, she caught a blur of pink. Michelle was marching toward Scott.

Sudi grabbed Michelle's arm before she could latch on to Scott. "Michelle's been dying to hook up with you," she said to Jeff. Spinning around, she playfully shoved Michelle into Jeff's arms.

Michelle glared at Sudi, then smiled up at Jeff

and fanned her face with her hands. "It's too hot. I think I need to get a drink." She disappeared again.

Sudi pulled Meri over to the far wall. "Don't let a guy stampede you into doing more than you're ready to do," Sudi scolded. "You'll be sorry if you do."

"How did you know I was uncomfortable?" Meri asked.

"I know who your crush is. Even though Jeff thinks he's it, I know he's not," Sudi answered.

"You know?" Meri asked.

"Like Dalila and I haven't figured out that you're totally crushing on Abdel," Sudi said. "We were just waiting for you to say something."

"Why didn't you tell me I was being so obvious?" Meri ran her fingers through her hair. Then another thought came to her, and she felt ashamed and foolish. "Abdel must think I'm a total loser. I'll never be able to face him again."

"Yes, you will, and you'll get your kiss, too," Sudi answered confidently. "Come on, dance with us."

Sudi and Scott tried to pull Meri on to the

dance floor, but she eased back against the wall. She stared at the floor and started to zone with all the other rejects lined up beside her. If Abdel did know, then why hadn't he said something to her?

The music stopped abruptly, and she glanced up.

Michelle walked across the stage and tapped the mike. Feedback screeched across the room, and everyone covered their ears.

"Meri Stark has wanted to sing since she got here, but she's just too shy to take the stage on her own," Michelle yelled.

Meri's eyes widened. She gazed at Michelle, unable to believe what she was doing.

Everyone standing near Meri turned and looked at her, with huge, silly smiles.

"Let's give it up for Meri," Michelle squealed and began clapping.

Kids whistled and hooted. Hands were everywhere, pushing, pulling, prodding her toward the stage.

"Let's see you handle this," Michelle said as she handed Meri the mike.

"Michelle, you're going to feel worse if you make me sing," Meri warned. "You don't want to do this."

"Please," Michelle answered. "Why would *I* feel bad if *you* make a fool of yourself? Pick out your song."

Meri scrolled through the list, then punched in the numbers for a ballad she had sung back in California. She'd never told anyone that she'd been in a girl band. They'd even recorded a demo, *Bust My Heart*, which had been a hit on the local radio stations until her mother's campaign advisers had decided that it wasn't decent for the daughter of a presidential hopeful to sing about lust.

The music started. Pounding drums shook the walls, marking out the beat. Meri could feel the tension rising in the audience.

Michelle stood next to Brian. The two of them snickered and made faces.

Sudi held up her hands to show Meri her crossed fingers.

Meri closed her eyes and belted out the first note. The purity of the tone rose in the room. She finished singing the first few lines and looked at the crowd. Kids started dancing. Others edged closer to the stage and gazed up at her.

Slowly, she scanned the crowd. She loved to perform.

Then she saw Abdel and her heart took on a quicker rhythm.

He stood alone in the middle of the dancers, watching her. He wore a crazy porkpie hat that was different from his usual conservative style, and a slouchy gray coat that made her want to laugh. She wondered if he had dressed that way for her.

For the first time since she'd met him, his expression was unguarded, and she recognized the longing in his gaze; she had seen it on other faces when she performed.

Maybe he did like her.

She sang in a soft, low voice, crooning about love, and imagined his arms around her.

Gradually, she became aware that others were looking in the direction of her gaze. She had been so infatuated with Abdel that she had forgotten her audience. She pulled her mind back to her performance, but in her nervousness, she forgot the lyrics. That had never happened before. She stammered and foolishly tried to fill in with *la-la-la*s.

Brian laughed, and Michelle grinned triumphantly.

Meri hummed, distraught, and felt the heat of a blush rising to her cheeks. She looked down at the prompter, but she couldn't find her place, and when she thought she had, she sang the wrong words.

She set the mike in its stand and ran off the stage.

Kids clapped, stamped their feet, and yelled out their praise, some calling for her to come back and sing more. But she felt woozy from nerves and leaned against the wall, afraid that if she didn't hold on to something, she'd lose her balance and fall.

Dalila and Sudi joined her

"Why did you run off the stage?" Sudi asked. "You have an incredible voice."

"Everyone loved your singing," Dalila agreed, hugging her. "You should go back and sing another song."

Meri shook her head. "I think I'd better go home."

"Abdel came here for a reason," Sudi said, seeming to read her mind.

"Yeah," Meri said. "He came here to check out The Jackal." She pressed her fingers over her eyes. "I can't believe I made such a fool of myself in front of everyone."

"He came here to see you," Dalila reassured her. "Ask him to dance. He's probably as shy as you are."

"Maybe you'll get your first kiss," Sudi teased and nudged Meri playfully.

"I'll show you my secret for regaining composure." Dalila took Meri's hand and forced the fingers into a fist. "Now, tap on your breastbone, smile, and think of someone you love."

"You're not serious," Meri said.

"I warned you that you'd laugh at me if I shared one of my secrets with you," Dalila said. "It's called the thymus thump, and it's been proven to revitalize your energy. Say 'ha-ha-ha' with each tap."

Meri shrugged, then stroked her breastbone with quick, light blows, feeling foolish as she recited the "ha-ha-ha." But she did feel better.

"It works," she said, startled.

"Now, go," Sudi said, pushing her onto the jammed dance floor.

Kids smiled at Meri and complimented her singing as she squeezed between them.

Then she saw Abdel, and her heart dropped.

He was dancing with Michelle.

CHAPTER 8

Michelle caught Meri's gaze and smiled wickedly as she worked her fingers over Abdel's shoulders. Then she raised one eyebrow and mouthed the word *mine*.

After that, she pulled his head down toward hers and closed her eyes, parting her lips in anticipation.

Meri wasn't going to watch Michelle steal the kiss that should have been her own. She elbowed past the dancers, frantic to leave, and rushed outside before anyone could see her tears.

She charged down the sidewalk, expecting the pop of a paparazzi flash to blind her.

When nothing happened, she kicked off her sandals and ran wildly, her feet slapping against the cold concrete. She let her tears come.

A car engine started.

She glanced over her shoulder. She couldn't bear to have photographers stalking her. She darted across the street and hid in an alley, behind some empty mango and pear crates.

An SUV rolled past her. Thimble sat in the driver's seat, one hand on the steering wheel, the other holding his camera, ready to shoot.

When the car turned at the corner, she started jogging again, ignoring the stares of people watching her through restaurant windows.

She had gone only a few blocks when lightning streaked across the sky. Moments later, a thunderclap shattered the night. The boom reverberated down the street, setting off car alarms.

Clouds formed, billowing and growing with

uncanny speed, and soon the rain came, splashing into puddles left over from the last storm.

As she neared her house, the night took on a sinister feel. She quickened her pace, wanting nothing more than to be home, cuddled in bed with a glass of milk and a handful of cookies, reading and—

Something moved in the deeper shadows near the house just ahead.

Fear swept through her.

Instinct told her to run, but when she looked again, she saw nothing in the gloomy night that should have made her feel so afraid.

Wind whipped through the trees, lashing branches back and forth, and making gray shadows swirl.

Maybe a photographer was stealthily following her, hoping to get a picture of her running in the rain, barefoot, wet, and shivering in her skimpy California clothes.

But fear also made her senses sharper; if someone were stalking her, surely she'd have been able to hear him prowling through the wet shrubs and grass. She paused and tilted her head, concentrating, but the rain hid any noise someone trailing her might have made.

Even so, her feeling of danger did not go away.

Cautiously, she stepped backward. Her ability to change into a cat had also given her the feline instincts to sense a predator.

Something brushed against her leg. She cried out and turned, ready to fight.

Three cats wagged their tails, their fur drenched and clinging to their thin, trembling bodies.

She fell to her knees, and by an odd telepathy, sensed their rising terror.

"What is it?" she asked, knowing they couldn't understand her question.

And then, with a shock that made adrenaline race through her blood, she knew that an ancient evil had been slinking after her and hiding in the shadows near the houses.

The cats had seen the twisting snake and had come to warn her.

"Apep?" she whispered. No sooner had the name come into her mind than the cats scurried away, bellies low to the ground in fear.

At the same moment the stormy night filled with the scent of cucumbers and mold.

Meri stood and stepped between two cars parked near the curb. Runoff waters rushed over her feet. She willed her body to change, but not all the way. Whiskers prickled through her cheeks. Then, in a burst, her feline vision came.

The demon Apep swept toward her, leaving a trail of greenish foam in his wake. The snake had become larger; he was the size of an anaconda that could easily wrap around her chest and squeeze until she couldn't draw a breath.

The serpent opened his mouth, fangs exposed, tongue flickering, and shrieked as lightning seared across the night.

Apep flailed his tail, coiling eagerly toward her at a speed that seemed impossible.

She froze, trying to decide what to do. She couldn't outrun the creature as she was, but if she changed into a cat, she could climb a tree and flee across the rooftops.

Still watching Apep, she backed into the street and began reciting the incantation to change. She stepped onto the next curb.

Apep followed her. The sound of his scales scraping over the pavement became louder than the pounding rain, the rhythm quicker.

Meri concentrated and intoned the spell again. She moved on to her neighbor's lawn, near a tree. Her clothing disappeared, and she stood naked in the rain before black fur covered her.

The muscles in her back quivered; she began to shrink. When she was able to open her cat eyes, Apep was only two feet away, his fetid breath steaming around her.

The snake struck.

She jumped to one side and hissed.

The serpent's fangs caught in the wet ground. It furiously thrashed about, trying to break free from the mud.

Meri scrambled up the tree and crouched. She scanned the lawn below. Leaves and branches waved in front of her, making it impossible to see clearly. Still, she should have seen some trace of the snake. Where had he gone?

The tree swayed, and at first she thought the wind had made the movement. Then she looked down. The reptile had curled himself around the trunk and was spiraling toward her, his lurid green eyes hungry and focused on her.

Her heart pounded fiercely. She leapt to the roof of the nearby house, but rain had made the pitched slope slick and she slid backward, catching herself in the rain gutter.

Wind lashed around her. She struggled to keep her balance.

A flash of lightning startled her.

She lost her grip and fell, twisting and turning, to land on her paws. She hit the soggy ground, then shot off and raced down the street as Apep uncurled himself from the tree.

Thunder rumbled around her, making her ears ache. She sped to her front porch and desperately tried to change back into a girl. She sensed that Apep wouldn't be able to follow her inside.

She concentrated. Her bones ached, and her tendons quivered, but she remained a cat.

The sickening smell of Apep filled the air. The hair on her back rose in little spikes.

She turned and faced the demon. As she tried to decide whether to fight or try to outrun it again, someone picked her up.

She hissed and clawed, thrashing about, struggling to break free.

Whoever held her petted her, trying to calm her. She could feel the transformation starting, becoming stronger than her ability to hold it back. She couldn't let the person holding her witness her change.

She twisted violently as her bones began to stretch. Her fur dissolved, and slick, wet skin grew around her hands and arms. She had transformed.

The night spun dizzily around her.

The person holding her caught her before she fell.

Unexpectedly, Apep bellowed and turned away, but the hands holding Meri didn't let go.

Anyone but a cult member would have fainted or screamed when she changed. Apep hadn't been trying to capture her after all. The ancient demon had been chasing her toward the cult member waiting for her at home.

Defeated, Meri turned to face her captor.

The cloudburst ended, and the night filled with the sound of gushing water. Rooftops and trees shed the downpour, filling drainpipes and gutters. The lush fragrance of wet earth and grass scented the air but Meri still tasted fear.

"At least let me see your face," she grumbled and kicked. Her bare foot brushed over a pant leg and hit the porch step, jamming her toes. Pain shot up her leg.

"Soul of Egypt," a voice soothed. "Why are you still fighting me?" The hands released her.

Meri looked up and gasped. Abdel stared down at her. She had been rescued, not captured.

"You saved me," she said. Tension drained from her arms and legs, leaving her light-headed and weak. "How did you make Apep leave?"

"The demon's not yet strong enough to fight us both," he replied, "but soon he will be."

"Us?" Meri gazed up at him. "You did it. I couldn't—"

Abdel placed the tips of his fingers on her lips to quiet her. "You didn't need me," he explained. "You would have won this encounter."

"I doubt it," Meri said and started to shiver.

Abdel placed his hands on her shoulders. With a start she realized he was touching bare skin. Terror had consumed her, and she hadn't noticed that her lacy tunic and bra hadn't made the transition with her. She quickly crossed her arms over her chest.

She felt hot tears of embarrassment sting her eyes.

Abdel took off his coat and slipped it over her shoulders.

"I can't believe you saw me," she said, shaking her head.

"You're beautiful," he whispered and tentatively placed his hands around her face. "Why did you leave the party?"

She stared into his eyes. How could she tell him that she had been jealous of Michelle?

"I wish you had stayed," he whispered. "I wanted to dance with you."

Her mouth opened, but her brain couldn't find the words to speak.

"I think I know why you left," he said.

"You do?" she asked.

"You saw me with Michelle," he answered.

Meri felt her heart drop.

"Michelle kissed me, but I didn't kiss her," he said. "I pulled away from her, but then you were gone. She was trying to make you jealous."

"If you knew that, then why did you dance with her?" Meri asked.

Abdel hesitated. "I saw you with someone," he confessed. "Michelle said his name

{ 101 }

was Jeff and that you liked him."

"I don't," Meri protested. "Michelle just wants to make my life miserable."

Abdel leaned down, his lips close to hers. Her heart raced with excitement.

She held her face up to his, anticipating his touch.

But then he hesitated, inches from her mouth.

Her mind whirled. Did he expect her to give him permission? She didn't know. All her friends had kissed guys, some had done more, but Meri had never asked for the details. Now she wished she had.

"It's okay," she whispered in a jagged voice, feeling suddenly too dizzy to stand.

He pulled back. "What is okay?"

"Kiss me before I faint," she said. Her heart lurched and skipped a beat.

He smiled. Then he closed his eyes and pressed his lips to hers.

She sighed, and her eyes widened. She wanted to remember everything about this kiss; the gentle ache of longing for him, the loving caress of his fingers on her temples and cheeks.

The kiss was over before she wanted it to be.

He pulled back and opened his eyes. A smile broke out across his face.

"You're supposed to close your eyes," he said, playfully shaking her shoulders.

"Of course, I know to close my eyes," she answered.

"Then why didn't you?" he asked.

She couldn't tell him that she had wanted to savor her first kiss.

"You've never kissed a guy before," he said softly. "I forgot that."

Her mind reeled. "Did Sudi tell you?"

"Of course not," he said. "Why would I talk to her about us?"

"Us?" she asked; and just as happiness started to buzz through her, another thought intruded. "Was the kiss that bad?" she asked. Then without pausing, she answered her own question. "That's how you knew it was my first time," she exclaimed. "Because the kiss was so terrible."

She pulled away from Abdel and rubbed her temples. She wished now that she had practiced kissing on the back of her hand or with pillows, as her friends had.

"Don't be upset," Abdel said. He tried to place his arms around her.

Meri jerked away from him, then fumbled in her skirt pocket, pulled out her key, pushed around Abdel, and unlocked the front door.

"What's wrong?" he asked.

She kept her head down, too embarrassed to look at him, and darted into the house.

"Good night." She slammed the door.

Abdel knocked. "Meri, at least talk to me. I didn't mean to upset you. I thought you wanted to kiss me."

"I do. I did," she said to the dark living room.

A miserable heaviness settled inside her. She leaned against the door and wiped her tears. She had wanted her first real kiss to be hearts-and-roses beautiful, a moment to remember for the rest of her life.

"Meri," Abdel called to her through the door.

"Go away," she said. She couldn't face him. She headed for the kitchen and opened the cupboard, pulled out a candy bar, tore off the wrapper, and took a big bite. Chocolate melted over her tongue.

She leaned against the counter and started to take off Abdel's jacket. Something rustled in the right pocket. She felt inside of it and pulled out an envelope. Her name was written across the front.

He hadn't actually given it to her, so maybe she should just leave it. She hesitated, then opened it anyway.

Divine one,

Isis has sent her burning love fires to me, and all I think about is you. Even with potions and spells I am unable to stop this love that consumes me. What will happen if I make a fatal error because my mind is clouded with love? Worse, I fear that you do not share my feelings, because you act so strangely when I am near. You turn your face away as if you can't bear the sight of me. I have decided to return to Egypt. A new mentor will be sent.

Fondly,
Abdel

"No," Meri screamed, surprised at the depth of her emotions.

She ran through the house, opened the front door, and sprinted down the front walk, splashing through the puddles.

At the corner, she stopped and looked both ways.

When she didn't see Abdel, she yelled into the night, "I love you!"

Her words echoed around her, and she knew he was gone.

CHAPTER 10

On Monday morning, Meri threaded her way among the guys clustered in small groups in front of the academy. She sipped her caffe latte, wishing she had added sugar to the bitter brew, and thought about Abdel. He hadn't responded to her e-mails or her text messages. Twice she had gone over to his house, but no one had answered the door.

A low snickering made her pause. She looked at the group of guys standing in front of her. Why were they all staring at her with such dreamy smiles?

"Hi, Meri," Cecil said, and nervously patted his black hair as if he were trying to impress her.

A chorus of hellos followed from the guys standing with him.

"Good morning," Meri answered, unsure why they were watching her.

They turned and stared at her as she headed up the front steps.

Michelle stood near the door, a stack of newspapers flung over her arm. She handed a copy of the *National Enquirer* to each student who entered the school. Gray newsprint covered her fingers; the tips of her French-manicured nails were tinged with black.

"Hi, Meri," she said with too much glee in her voice. She had rimmed her lids with silver, and her sapphire eyes looked brighter.

"What's up?" Meri asked. "It's spooky the way everyone looks so happy."

"You're front-page news," Michelle said with a wicked grin and handed Meri a paper.

The cup slipped from Meri's hand. Hot coffee splattered Michelle's legs and soaked into Meri's socks and shoes, but Meri didn't notice the burn.

"Ouch!" Michelle jumped back and hit the door with a loud bang. "You did that on purpose!"

Meri didn't answer. She stared down at the paper. Someone had followed her and taken her picture as she had transformed. In the first photo, she was walking in the rain, her wet clothes clinging to her body. In the second, she stood under the tree, completely nude as the change started. A flash of lightning had apparently blurred the third shot and, thankfully, it was impossible to make out her whiskers, tail, and shrinking size.

"What's up?" Scott asked, tugging the paper from Meri. His spicy cologne filled the brisk morning air.

"Dang." He glanced at Meri's boxy school jacket. "You should definitely wear tighter clothes."

"She probably posed for the picture," Michelle said. "Can you imagine anyone doing that?"

Scott chuckled. "Michelle, you're not going to win with this one," he said. "Meri looks drop-dead gorgeous."

"She's naked!" Michelle countered.

"Ye-e-e-a-a-ah," Scott said, stretching the word

out in a slow, easy way as he gazed down at the picture again.

"I hate you, Meri!" Michelle stormed inside, but not before Meri grabbed the remaining newspapers from her.

Meri bundled them up and hurried down the steps, ignoring the comments from the guys. When she was far enough away from school, she pitched the papers in a trash bin, keeping two copies. Then she ran out into the street and hailed a cab, already texting a message to Sudi.

Three hours later, Sudi, Dalila, and Meri sat in Meri's bedroom puzzling over the photographs in the *Enquirer*. Sudi had ditched her afternoon classes, and Dalila had had to climb out her bedroom window in order to avoid the bodyguard that her uncle had hired to protect her from the cult.

Dalila kicked off her jeweled thong sandals and leaned against the pillows on Meri's bed, engrossed in looking at the photos.

"A photographer must have followed you when you left The Jackal," Sudi said, gazing down at the paper that she and Meri shared. She looked up again and studied Meri. "No wonder the guys were gawking at you. I mean, you always look so tomboy, and you're really incredible. You should borrow some of my clothes and flaunt yourself a little more. My green—"

"Let's get back to the problem." Meri nervously brushed her fingers through her hair.

"Wow," Sudi said again.

Meri felt a blush rising.

"Your concentration would have been on Apep," Dalila said, "so it's possible you didn't see a photographer."

"I was looking at Apep," Meri added, "so whoever took my picture would have seen the snake, too, and should have been too terrified to take my picture."

"Unless one of the freelance photographers who chases after you has joined the cult," Sudi said. "Maybe the cameraman was hoping to get a more gruesome photo. You know, 'Giant D.C. Snake Eats Girl.'"

Meri shuddered. "I don't like that idea at all."

Dalila crinkled her copy of the paper, then spread it on top of the one that Meri and Sudi had been studying. "I think we have a bigger problem."

She pointed to another article on page three. "Tourists are disappearing near the FDR Memorial," Dalila said. "The memorial is next to the Tidal Basin, and bodies of water have always been entrances to the Netherworld."

"Do you think that's the way Apep is going back and forth to his lair?" Meri asked.

"I'm certain it is," she answered. "We need to find Abdel."

"That could be a problem," Meri said and fell back onto her bed. "I have something to confess."

By the time Meri had finished telling them everything that had happened between her and Abdel, she and her friends had eaten three bags of microwave popcorn and had gone downstairs to the kitchen to start on the chocolate-chip cookies that Georgie had baked before going home.

"We don't have time to wait for a new mentor to find us," Dalila said, frowning.

"You're right," Sudi agreed. "I think we should destroy Apep before he kills more tourists."

"Abdel said not to do anything until he found a protective spell," Meri countered.

"He deserted us," Dalila said with a flash of anger.

"It's my fault," Meri said guiltily.

"He's the mentor," Dalila corrected. "He should know better than to leave us, especially now."

"I agree." Sudi dipped her cookie in a glass of milk. "So how are we going to stop Apep?"

"According to legend, Apep must be dismembered until each bone in his body is separated from the rest," Dalila explained.

"Gross." Sudi set her cookie on a napkin. "That's disgusting. I can't do that. I can't even kill garden snails for my mother. I don't have the stomach to—" She didn't finish her sentence and grimaced.

"Can't we just look in the Book of Thoth?" Meri asked, feeling ill just from imagining getting close enough to Apep to cut through his scales. "Abdel was going to find a spell. So maybe we can."

"Besides, how can we slaughter something as big as an anaconda?" Sudi asked. "We'll have a thousand witnesses and probably become the lead story on the local news."

"We'll do it on Halloween night," Dalila said

calmly. "Then, if anyone sees what we're doing, they'll think it's only holiday shenanigans."

"I've never heard of anyone cutting up a snake on Halloween," Sudi answered.

"It's not exactly a holiday tradition," Meri agreed unhappily.

"The only problem is that we'll need to find sacred knives," Dalila said. She looked at the ceiling as if she were mentally going through museum displays. "Have you seen any in the Smithsonian?"

"You don't expect us to steal something from the Smithsonian, do you?" Meri asked.

"We're supposed to stand against evil," Dalila replied.

"I know we're supposed to do whatever it takes," Sudi said, "but we'll get caught. There's no way."

"All right," Dalila said reluctantly, "I'll look through my uncle's catalog of artifacts. Maybe he has something that he's studying now. Hopefully, he has borrowed a few knives from a museum that we can use."

"I've got to go home," Sudi said as she started for the front door. "Mom's planned a family night."

She shook her head. "Abdel chose the wrong person when he picked me over my sisters. They love this kind of weird stuff."

"He didn't do the choosing," Dalila said, correcting her. "Fate did, when the birthmark was given to you."

Sudi sighed. "Just my luck." She turned at the door and looked back at Meri. "I'm scared."

"Me, too," Meri replied.

Dalila didn't say anything. Tears rimmed her eyes.

Meri hugged them each good-bye.

After Sudi and Dalila left, Meri went back to the kitchen to rinse out their milk glasses. *Washingtonian* magazine lay open on the counter.

Fear raced up her spine. The magazine hadn't been there before. She would have noticed it. She walked over to it and stared down at a full-page advertisement for the Anubis Spa, announcing the opening of a special exhibit of ancient Egyptian relics that included ritual knives.

$\mathcal{L}$

$\mathbf{M}$eri stood on the street corner, all attitude and tough demeanor, even though her heart was racing. She stared up at the Anubis Building, then lifted the huge sunglasses she had just bought from a vendor and scanned the block behind her to make sure no photographers had spotted her in spite of her disguise.

She had slicked back her hair and redefined her eyebrows—not that anyone was going to see her eyes—but the arch jutting over her brow did not look like her. Neither did the tailored pantsuit that Roxanne had picked out for her. She fiddled with the collar to make sure her pink T-shirt wasn't showing, and waited.

After a car passed, she crossed the street and prayed that no one saw the outline of the Bermuda shorts she wore under her slacks. She carried a computer case in which she had packed a cotton hat, flip-flops, a moist cloth, and her papyrus from the Book of Thoth. She hoped that anyone who saw her would think she was a college intern who worked in the congressional offices.

Black glass covered the building facade and reflected the line of orange school buses parked at the curb. The front door opened, and children burst outside, running past Meri and shouting to each other about mummies and cat coffins.

Meri hadn't told Dalila or Sudi about her plan. She sensed that the advertisement so boldly left on her kitchen counter had been more trick than invitation. She was probably heading into a trap. Still, she had to take the risk. They needed the knives to stop Apep.

She stepped into the lobby, clutching the strap of the computer case so no one would see her hands trembling, and walked with purposeful steps through the flow of children still exiting the building.

Moments later, she entered the exhibit hall. The lights were dim, other than those focused on the artifacts in the display cases. She started forward and nearly bumped into a man before she realized he was the spa owner.

Adrenaline shot through her, and her mouth went dry with fear.

She strode past him, her back twitching, and pretended to examine the canopic jars.

The sound of rhythmic clapping startled her. Rattles and drums joined the noise.

She stepped between two large sarcophagi as a parade of eager children marched past her. Some shook sistrums, and others beat on drums. Those who didn't have instruments clapped and jumped. Their teacher beamed, enjoying their excitement.

Two security guards followed the group into the room. The larger one, with sunburned cheeks, checked his watch.

Meri turned her face away and pretended to read a plaque describing a blue glass headrest.

When the guards passed, she hurried down a hallway to the next exhibit room. She had gone only a few steps when she heard someone behind her. She turned abruptly.

Her sudden movement startled two young boys who had been creeping up behind her, probably bored with the artifacts and playing at being spies. They laughed and ran back to the first room.

Meri walked past more display cases, her urgency building. She sensed she was running out of time, and still she had not found the knives.

Then a distant voice spoke. ". . . The ancient Egyptians valued tranquility and order. . . ."

A guide was bringing another group of children through.

Meri needed to steal the knives and leave before the tour caught up to her. She quickened her pace.

In the next row, knives with slashing blades and lotus-flower handles sat in a display, along with jewel-encrusted daggers made from gold, bronze, and lapis lazuli.

She bent closer, studying the hieroglyphs engraved in the metal, until her breath fogged the glass. Then she saw what she wanted. A knife with a long, scalloped blade and an alabaster handle carved in the form of the fierce war goddess Sekhmet. Her name meant "the powerful one," and her fury was so devastating that other gods had had to intervene to save humankind from her destruction.

Meri looked around the room. She didn't see anyone, not even a security guard. That struck her as odd, but she couldn't think about it at the moment.

She shut the doors, closing the only entrance into the room other than an emergency exit, and quickly slipped a dead bolt into place.

She raced back to the display, unzipped the computer case, and pulled out the papyrus. Her heart pounded as she stared down at the spell she intended to use.

Both Dalila and Abdel had cautioned her about calling forth the goddess Sekhmet. Invoking her name could unleash terrifying power.

Meri closed her eyes and lifted her arms.

"Now I speak the terrible name Sekhmet," she

whispered, "and call forth her power. Open the seal, that I might have the knives to protect the world from the fiend Apep."

Then she read from the scroll. *"Behen a Sebau, se hetem na Apep,"* she intoned. "May I crush the evil one, may I destroy Apep."

Hot desert winds blew into the room, flapping her suit jacket as the scorching gust whirled around her.

The lioness-headed goddess appeared in a storm of sand, and with uncanny grace she walked over to the knife display and opened it.

The goddess vanished, and someone began screaming.

Meri whipped around.

The two boys who had followed her before stared at her, their faces covered with sand, screeching.

"No one is going to hurt you," Meri said, trying to reassure them. "Please be quiet."

When she lifted the knives from the display, an alarm went off. She clenched her jaw, bracing herself against the ear-piercing sound, and dropped the knives into her computer case. Shouting came from the hallway. The locked door shook as people on the other side banged against it, trying to break into the room. The boys ran to the door, sobbing and crying for help.

Meri set the papyrus on top of the knives, closed the case, and hurried across the room. She slammed through the emergency exit and rushed into a narrow passageway between the buildings. The stench of garbage was overwhelming.

She threw off her sunglasses, stepped out of her heels, and tore off her suit as sirens became louder than the alarms. With trembling fingers, she snapped her computer case open, grabbed the cotton sun hat and set it on her head, then yanked out the canvas tote and jammed the knives and papyrus inside it. Quickly she set her flip-flops on the ground, stepped into them, and grabbed the cloth. She left the computer case and ran toward the street, scrubbing off her fake eyebrows. Barely able to breathe, she turned the corner.

The alarms stopped, but her ears continued ringing.

At last she eased into the crowd that had gathered in front of the Anubis Building. She now wore the loose pink T and Bermuda shorts that she had worn under the suit and looked like any high school girl who had come to the District on her senior trip to the capital.

Something trickled across her palm. She looked down and saw her blood spattered on the sidewalk. She had cut her finger on one of the blades. Feeling dizzy, she wrapped the cut in the tail of her T-shirt. She needed to sit down before she fainted.

Her knees trembled, but she remained standing and mentally went back over what she had done. She had never had her fingerprints taken, so the impressions she had left behind could never lead the detectives to her. She had removed the labels from the pantsuit, so the clothing left in the alley wouldn't provide a clue. The computer case had been purchased at a garage sale in California: another dead end.

But the theft had been too easy, and that nagged at her. The priceless artifacts had been left unguarded, and that led her to only one conclusion. The cult wanted her to have the knives.

CHAPTER 12

The rain had stopped, and the thunderous gray clouds had drifted away, leaving the night air moist and smelling of wet leaves. Halloween revelers paraded up and down Embassy Row, carrying trick-or-treat bags and eating candy.

Meri, Dalila, and Sudi walked away from the Australian embassy, clutching candy, and joined the throng, mostly college students, in costumes.

"Did you see the way that woman stared at

your whiskers?" Sudi said and brushed her hand over the cat ears poking through Meri's hair.

A pleasant feeling rushed through Meri, and a low rumble rose in her throat. She pushed Sudi's hand away.

"Be careful," Meri warned. "You almost made me purr."

"You need to purr," Sudi countered. "You're too nervous."

"Aren't you?" Meri asked. "I'm so jittery I could puke."

Instead of trying to hide the whiskers, tail, or feline ears that appeared when she was nervous, Meri had decided at the last moment to pull on a black leotard and dress as a cat. She wore a black velvet sash that held the Sekhmet knife close to her waist.

"But you stole the knives," Dalila said. "That's braver than I could ever be."

The wind caught Dalila's blue-silk veils and lifted them into the air, exposing the jewel-encrusted knife handle that lay flat against her smooth skin. The blade was tucked into the sequined band of her low-slung belly dancer's skirt.

"Great costume," said a guy dressed as a pirate.

In response, Dalila struck her finger cymbals. The brass plates pinged as she twirled with elegant grace. The skirt and veils swirled around her.

"I can't believe you did that," Sudi teased. "I'm the party girl."

"At least Dalila and I wore costumes," Meri scolded playfully. "I thought the plan was to look like trick-or-treaters in case someone caught us."

"I'm a tango dancer," Sudi said. With a sharp turn of her head, she embraced an invisible partner and took slow, slinking steps down the sidewalk, threading her way among kids dressed as witches, ghosts, and cheerleaders.

At the corner, Sudi did a quick foot flick through the slit in her skirt, revealing the ancient Egyptian knife, hooked into a lacy red garter that she wore above her knee.

Meri and Dalila laughed and ran up to her.

"Shouldn't we go to the Tidal Basin?" Dalila asked, gathering her veils tightly around her.

"I guess," Meri answered reluctantly.

Sudi grabbed their arms. "We have to stop at the Peruvian embassy first," Sudi said. "It's just across the street, and last year they gave out these incredible chocolate bars called Sublimes. We're not leaving until we each get one."

But as she started to step off the curb, a rusted old Cadillac rumbled down Massachusetts Avenue.

"That's Brian's car," Sudi whispered.

"So?" Meri asked.

"Why does he always show up wherever I am?" Sudi asked, looking after the car. Black smoke curled from the tailpipe.

"Maybe because you go to the same school and hang out with the same friends," Meri offered.

"No, it's not just coincidence," Sudi whispered with a haunted look. "It's something more."

"Why are you still afraid of Brian?" Dalila asked.

"I'm not," Sudi snapped. She scowled and started walking back the way they had come, her heels tapping out a fast, angry pace.

Meri and Dalila silently followed her down Sixteenth Street. No one spoke until they reached Lafayette Park and stood in front of the White House.

Then the strange mood Brian had cast over Sudi lifted, and her lively energy returned.

"When you're living there, Meri, we'll hang out, and watch all the cute Secret Service guys." Sudi hung her arm over Meri's shoulder. "My parents think your mom will win."

"She has to get the nomination first," Meri countered.

"Invite us for tea," Dalila added. "Can you imagine how elegant everything will be?" She clasped Meri's hand. "State dinners! You'll be entertaining kings."

Meri nodded but then she glanced up at the roof and saw the silhouette of a man. Since President Clinton had been in office, sharpshooters had kept watch from the White House roof. Meri's mother had already received death threats. Meri wondered what it would be like if she actually won the office.

Twenty minutes later, the girls stood on the western edge of the Tidal Basin, near the Franklin Delano Roosevelt Memorial. Moonlight reflected across the waters, and the rising tide made waves wash against the concrete and stone bank with a gentle whisper.

"Only a few visitors are walking around the

memorial," Sudi said. "I think most of the tourists are celebrating Halloween."

Meri glanced behind the gnarled trunks of the old cherry trees. Just one tour bus waited in the parking lot that was normally full.

"How do we even know Apep is here?" Meri asked.

"Since your last encounter with him, I've been keeping track of the storms," Dalila replied. "The thunder and rain this afternoon brought him into our world. He hasn't left yet."

"Do you think he's waiting for us?" Meri asked.

Sudi pointed into the dark behind the park bench. The wire-mesh fence had been twisted and bent until it was flattened against the ground. On the other side of the trees, the wooden slats of the second fence lay broken and scattered about the parking lot.

"Apep couldn't have done that," Meri argued, trying to ignore the ominous feeling building inside her. "A car must have plowed through the fences and plunged into the water."

"Then why aren't the trees crushed, too?"

Dalila asked. She set her finger cymbals down and unwound her veils, then tied them around a low-hanging branch. The wind whipped the silky scarves high into the air.

Dalila pulled out her knife, her eyes serious. She kissed the blade and whispered an incantation. She didn't look afraid.

"We should probably split up," Sudi said, slipping the knife from her garter. She held it as if she knew how to use the weapon.

"Shout if you find Apep," Sudi joked, with an unfamiliar catch in her voice.

"I'll scream, more likely," Meri said glumly as she headed south, walking away from her friends to the far end of the memorial.

A thin mist settled over the ground, leaving tiny droplets on the grass. The dew reflected the moon's glow and shimmered with eerie beauty. Meri studied the dark shadows around the back of the memorial and wished she had brought a flash-light.

A dry rustle came from behind the furrowed trunk of a weather-beaten tree.

Anxious, Meri crept toward the sound, her

heartbeat pounding in her ears. She clutched the knife handle in her clammy palm, tightening her grip, and stared down, searching for the snake.

Cautiously, she peered behind the trunk and then let out a long sigh.

A discarded lunch bag flapped back and forth, crackling as the brown paper brushed against dead leaves.

Meri breathed deeply and pressed her hand over her jittery stomach.

The slap-slap rhythm of a jogger made her wary; a lone man was running down the walkway, his cap pulled low over his forehead.

Meri slid behind a tree and waited for the runner to pass. She didn't want someone who might recognize her to see her skulking around the cherry trees, clutching a sharp-bladed, lethal knife.

Abruptly, the pounding footsteps stopped. She wondered why the runner had paused.

Minutes passed. Finally, Meri looked out. She didn't see anyone on the walk or resting in the grass. Maybe the runner had moved on.

Curious, she stepped forward. She had gone only a short distance when she saw a gray lump, no bigger than a squirrel, on the sidewalk. As she neared it, she realized it was a tennis shoe. She picked it up. The lining was still warm, the sole covered with a strange stickiness. She dropped the shoe. It bounced once and fell into the pool.

A soft scraping sound filled the night. The noise increased, then fell back, only to start again.

Maybe the runner had fallen and was dragging himself over dead grass and leaves, trying to find help. But even as her mind tried to override her fear and find a logical explanation for the sound, her body reacted in a visceral way. A spasm shot up her back, and adrenaline raced through her.

As she started to turn, a shadow passed over her.

At first, she thought a cloud had raced across the sky, blocking the moonlight, but then the brisk autumn air became filled with a musty scent, after which came the rancid odor of decaying cucumbers.

Meri readied herself to attack, then spun around. She looked up, inhaling sharply, and froze.

Apep had tripled in size since the last time

Meri had seen him. The giant snake reared, extending himself until his head towered above Meri.

She stepped backward, stumbling over her own feet. Her cat ears, tail, and whiskers abandoned her, leaving her to deal with her terror as a regular girl, without any comfort from her feline powers.

The serpent's head angled over her; his mouth poised above her, fangs exposed, ready to strike.

A scream gurgled in her throat, then died.

The knife slipped from her sweating palm and landed in the grass with a soft plop. She fell to her knees, frantically brushing her hands across the ground, searching for the blade.

Before she could retrieve the knife, Apep struck.

She rolled, dodging the sudden thrust of the head, then stood, waiting; when Apep drew back to strike again, she ran forward and ducked under his body.

Her hands squished against his scaly underbelly. The snake came down hard on top of her. She screamed in pain and twisted free, turning over and over until she had gotten away from the beast.

"Dalila! Sudi!" she shouted, but the words came out as no more than a puff of air. Her friends would never be able to hear her calls for help.

The foamy muck that Apep left in his trail covered her hands. Bile rose to the back of her throat. She swiped her fingers back and forth in the dew-wet grass, trying to get rid of the gluey slime.

Apep roared. The deep, prolonged cry thundered through the night.

Meri stood, trying to make her mind work and find a plan. She edged back, mentally scolding herself for not having the courage to face Apep. She had wanted to be fierce, like the goddess Sekhmet, rather than sniveling and afraid. Fate had chosen her to be a Descendant. She was supposed to be brave, but instead she was sick with terror.

Apep slunk closer, winding toward her, his piercing eyes trying to entrance her.

She took a clumsy step back, and her foot caught on a root. Her ankle turned. She lost her balance and fell down. Her head snapped back and hit the tree trunk. Pain shot up her spine. The soreness settled in her neck with a dull throb.

Apep hissed and slithered closer. The forked

tongue flicked in and out, darting up and down, tasting the air, a tracking device for locating prey. When it swiped over her face, she cried out. The tongue felt damp and left a sharp tingling on her skin.

The snake's mouth widened as his flexible lower jaw scooped up her feet. His fetid breath choked her, and the stench clung to her skin. She stared into the gaping mouth, down into the horrible darkness, and saw the jogger's cap.

A low and terrible moan escaped her lungs, her last desperate cry, as she watched the flicking tongue and imagined her death: swallowed, then suffocated as the reptile's digestive acids worked on her flesh.

CHAPTER 13

Slowly, Meri became aware of footsteps hammering the ground. Voices called her name. Sudi and Dalila grabbed her shoulders and, yelling savagely, yanked her from Apep's mouth. Their fingers dug into her shoulder and arm as they tugged harder. Her leotard ripped, and the sleeve unraveled as her back scraped over the rough tree bark. Pain raced through her, and cuts stung her back.

At last Sudi and Dalila pulled her to the other side of the tree.

Meri gratefully breathed the untainted air. "Thanks," she whispered in between coughs.

Enraged, Apep rose up. His jaws snapped violently around the tree. The trunk cracked and splintered. A branch fell. Twigs and leaves scratched Meri's face.

Dalila shoved the foliage away and fell down on her knees beside Meri. "You need to get up," she coaxed. "Apep will be coming after us."

Sudi let out a low whistle and handed Meri the knife with the Sekhmet handle. "You dropped this," she said, staring at the reptile. "No wonder. I thought you said Apep was the size of an anaconda."

"He grew," Meri said, choking back sobs.

The snake released the broken tree and bellowed, then slid toward them in smooth, wavelike motions, his scales glossy and white in the milky moonlight.

"He is huge," Sudi breathed.

"How did you know I was in trouble?" Meri asked as she got to her feet, weak and trembling.

"Your screams were a clue," Sudi answered. "We'd better get this done before the police get here."

"A queen must not show fear. . . ." Dalila muttered, trying to give herself courage. "She must always instill confidence and hope in her people." Then she turned to Meri and Sudi, a strange, blank look on her face. "We'll survive this," she said, but there was a question in her voice.

Meri looked down at her knife. The blade caught the moonlight and flashed with a supernaturally bright glow. "Even though Apep is evil, I hate doing this."

"There has to be another way," Sudi said.

"This is what is expected from us." Dalila stood taller and gripped the handle of her knife.

Meri took a deep breath and ran. An avalanche of fear sent adrenaline buzzing through her. Her feet hammered the ground, and she yelled as she attacked the snake. She dodged his thrashing head and continued running until she stood over his midsection. She plunged her knife into his glistening scales. As the blade cut through the reptile's body, the slick sound made her cringe.

Apep bellowed and thrust his tail, coiling it around Meri. She brought the blade down again, slicing through flesh.

The snake squeezed tighter, wrapping more coils around Meri. The pressure on her lungs made it impossible to breathe. Darkness pressed into her vision, and she became vaguely aware that Sudi and Dalila stood beside her, striking the reptile with heavy blows.

The tail went slack, and the beast squealed.

Meri took deep breaths and brought her knife down again. This time something warm splattered her face. She turned her mind from what she was doing and thought of Sekhmet. The goddess had been sent by the god Re to avenge evil for him. At his bidding, she had killed men and women until the slaughter became sweet to her heart and she waded about in their blood. For that reason and others, the goddess of destruction and war was a terrible force to summon.

Meri did so again.

"Behen a Sebau, se hetem na Apep," Meri intoned. "May I crush the evil one; may I destroy Apep."

The wind came as a soft murmur at first, the

hot air withering grass as it rushed across the Mall. The scorching gusts screeched around them and a pale image of the lioness-headed goddess appeared in the shadows, wavering over the slaughter and protecting the Descendants.

CHAPTER 14 ~

M eri sat on the walk, her feet dangling over the edge into the Tidal Basin. The tide was at its highest, the water lapping around her ankles. She leaned forward and washed her hands in the cold, soothing liquid. Wisps of blood looped and curled into the moonlit water before dissolving.

"No more," Meri whispered. Her arm throbbed, and a stiff, painful feeling in her neck and back made it hard for her to bend low enough to clean her face. "I can't do more."

"It's over," Sudi said, dunking her bare feet into the water to wash the dirt and muck from her legs.

They had dropped the ritual knives next to the dead snake and left the carnage for others to find. Already, Meri could hear cries of alarm in the distance.

"Someone must have discovered Apep," Dalila said. Her hair was matted, her clothes stuck to her body, but in the moonlight, Meri wasn't sure if it was blood that covered her or the sticky film from the demon's underbelly.

"I think we should leave," Dalila said, standing.

"All right," Meri said, but she didn't get up.

Dalila made a sound: a mutter of disgust. She sighed and covered her eyes. "What did we do?"

"I'll tell you what we did." Sudi jumped up, dripping water on Meri's head. "We killed a monster, and now we can party."

"Party?" Meri turned to look at Sudi.

"Maybe being the protectors of the world won't be so bad after all," Sudi said, trying to sound happy.

Meri pulled herself up and limped over to her friend. "Are you all right?"

"Of course I am," Sudi snapped.

A hellish scream made them turn, and then a gun fired.

"Why would they need a gun?" Meri asked. "Apep is dead, a thousand pieces—"

"There!" Sudi shouted.

Meri followed her gaze.

Apep moved toward the water's edge, restored and larger than before, his scales smooth and gleaming. He slithered over a park bench and then the chain-link fence. The metal supports creaked and groaned under the reptile's weight as the bars bent. The snake dragged the wire mesh over the walkway, with a terrible screech of metal.

He splashed into the pool, and in the same moment, lightning streaked across the night. Thunder crackled and smashed, the low rumble shaking the ground. Rounded masses of clouds swept in from the east and began building, piling one on top of the other until they hid the moon.

"It's just as I feared," Dalila said at last. "When

destroyed, many Egyptian gods and demons simply regenerated. Apep is stronger now."

"The cult leaders let me steal the knives," Meri added. "They were taunting us. They knew we couldn't destroy Apep."

"They haven't won," Sudi said, gripping Meri's hand. "There has to be another way. We just need to find it."

"But how many people will Apep destroy before then?" Dalila asked softly.

Lightning shot jaggedly across the sky, and the rain fell in large drops as thunder rocked the night again.

Meri, Dalila, and Sudi started walking in the rain, ignoring the groups of people who had gathered.

The voices faded behind them, and then there was only the sound of rain.

When they reached the area where the tourist buses parked, they saw a huge, rusted Cadillac. Brian got out and grinned, resting his arms on the roof. Rain pelted his face.

"Do you need a ride home?" he asked with a chuckle in his voice.

"Brian," Sudi said, "have you been following me?"

"Why would I be following you?" he smirked and looked at Meri. "I liked that picture of you in the newspaper."

Meri rolled her eyes.

"That's unbelievable Halloween makeup," he said, no longer gazing into her eyes. "Where did you get it?"

"CVS," Meri lied, glancing down at her tattered leotard.

"Let's get a cab," Meri said to Dalila and Sudi.

"Like this?" Sudi asked. "No one will give us a ride."

Dalila looked back at Brian. "How did he know where to find us?"

"Come on!" Brian yelled, his voice rising with impatience. "I'm getting wet."

"Maybe he's joined the cult and he's watching us for them," Sudi said in a harsh, low voice. "I don't know. What else could it be?"

"Let's play along with him," Dalila said. "He's here for a reason. Let's find out what it is." She walked over to the Cadillac with a saucy stride.

"Do you think he just wants to get back with you?" Meri whispered to Sudi.

"Not likely," Sudi replied as she followed Dalila.

"We'll get your car dirty." Dalila tossed Brian a flirty smile as she waited for him to open the passenger-side door for her.

"I can clean the car," he said, staring at her bare belly.

Dalila slid inside, letting her skirt ride up and expose her perfect legs. She glanced at Brian, watching him watch her, and didn't shy away from his gaze. Instead, she stretched and posed seductively.

"Where did she learn that stuff?" Sudi said in a low voice to Meri. "I wish I'd been homeschooled by her teachers."

"She's amazing, isn't she?" Meri agreed. "And she knows just what she's doing. I bet she'll get Brian to tell us what he knows and he won't even know he's blabbing."

Meri crawled into the back as Brian pushed in behind the steering wheel.

The car rolled away. Windshield wipers made

a slick sound across the windows, and then Brian turned on the stereo. A rhythmic, pounding vibrated through Meri. She could feel Brian watching her through the rearview mirror, and when she glanced up, he was staring at her. His gaze returned to the road, and they drove to her house without talking.

"Sudi, are you going to be okay?" Meri asked as she got out of the car.

"I'm safe." Sudi nodded. "Dalila's with me."

Then Sudi leaned forward and spoke to Brian, "Go to my house next."

The car sped away, red taillights reflecting off the rain-slick street, and turned at the corner.

Meri splashed through the puddles and hurried to the back of the house. She unlocked the door, entered, and punched in the security code, then stood for a moment in the warm air, letting the heat embrace her before she undressed.

She curled her wet leotard into a ball and dumped it in the trash, then stepped naked into the kitchen just as the electricity went out. She grabbed the box of emergency candles and headed upstairs, grateful that no one was home.

Georgie had cleaned the bathroom earlier, and the scent of Clorox took Meri's mind off the odor clinging to her. She lit a dozen candles, setting the bases in the wet wax she had dripped onto the rim of the sink, and then she took a shower by gleaming candlelight. She sat in the tub and let the spray wash over her head. She didn't want to comb out her hair and find a piece of snake flesh clinging to a strand.

By the time she was finished and stood dripping on the rug, the thunder had quieted and a plan was running through her mind. She stepped into her bedroom and glanced at the flashing display on her clock. The electricity had returned, but she wasn't sure of the time. Still, she felt certain she could walk to Abdel's house and return before her mother got home.

She reasoned that Abdel would not have taken the Book of Thoth with him. It would have served no purpose; the next mentor would only have to bring the scrolls back.

Before she had even thought her idea through, she was pulling on her sweats. She grabbed a book of matches and her house key, punched a code into the alarm panel, and headed out the door.

She jogged down the sidewalk, her tennis shoes smacking against the wet pavement.

The sky was clear again, the moonlight bright, but the strange stillness in the air promised another storm.

As she neared Abdel's house she slowed her pace and looked around. Eerie Halloween music played in an apartment building on the next block, and jack-o'-lanterns set out earlier still had candles flickering inside them in spite of the storm. But she didn't see anyone.

Still her nerves thrummed as she jumped up on Abdel's front porch. She reached across the railing to see if she could force open the window, but when she pressed her fingers against the glass, she caught something in the corner of her eye. She turned, surprised.

The front door was open.

She pushed against the wood, letting the door swing wide. It bumped against the wall.

Caution told her not to call out. She slipped inside and closed the door, then waited. When she didn't hear anyone inside the house, she crossed to the stairs and started up the steps, her breathing shallow and loud.

As she reached the third-floor landing, she paused again. A gentle movement of air brought the faint scent of smoke. Had someone just extinguished the wicks in the oil-burning lamps?

A clammy cold filled the hallway, but other than that and the smoke, she didn't hear or feel anything strange. She entered the room, struck a match, and lit the wick floating in the first bowl of oil. The fire flared, leaving a thin black mark on the wall.

Meri blew out the match and then turned, not prepared for what she saw.

Papyri from the Book of Thoth had been unrolled and stretched across the floor, as if someone had been in a panic to find a spell. Had Abdel done this before he left? He had been searching for an incantation to protect the Descendants from Apep, but Meri couldn't imagine that he would ever have treated the ancient writings so irreverently.

Another thought occurred to her: the cult leaders also wanted the papyri. Maybe she had interrupted someone who was trying to steal the sacred writings.

She didn't think her sudden appearance could have panicked a cult leader. But she didn't understand why a thief would unwind the scrolls and leave them in such a chaotic jumble when he could have just taken them.

A shadow moved. Meri became aware that someone was standing behind her.

CHAPTER 15

Adrenaline shot through Meri, preparing her exhausted body to fight. She turned around and grabbed her neck. "Ouch!" she yelled, rubbing the tender muscles.

Tiny red eyes gazed back at her from the dark corner. Then chirping filled the room, and a bird with an elegant, S-shaped neck waddled toward her, its blunt claws clattering on the hardwood floor. A long, daggerlike beak opened, and a loud trill came out. Meri covered her ears.

"Sudi?" Meri asked.

The flapping wings turned into graceful arms, and the bird grew taller. Sudi appeared. She wore clean jeans and a boy tank. Her wet hair was pulled back in braids. She hugged Meri, and the musky fragrance of her shampoo filled the air.

Meri's tension eased, and she let out a huge sigh.

A tweet escaped Sudi's mouth. She coughed and tried again. "You scared us to death," she said, brushing fine, fluffy feathers from her arms.

"Where's Dalila?" Meri asked. She looked at the shadows hovering near the back wall.

A cobra slid forward, twisting and curling until it stood on the tip of its tail; then, still whirling, its body thickened, and Dalila appeared, spinning out of control.

Sudi and Meri grabbed her and stopped her from hitting her forehead against the bookshelves.

Dalila pressed her hands on either side of her head. "I'm so dizzy," she said. "I think I'm going to be sick." She wore Sudi's clothes: a denim miniskirt with a pink baby-doll top and flip-flops.

"At least you didn't become that devourer monster with the big butt when you transformed," Sudi said. She turned her attention back to Meri. "We asked Brian to leave us both at my house," Sudi explained. "My parents and sisters are still at a Halloween party, and Dalila couldn't let her uncle see—"

"—What a mess I'd become," Dalila said. "Besides, I didn't want to be alone in the car with Brian. His behavior is unacceptable."

Meri raised an eyebrow and glanced sideways at Sudi. "Translation?"

"He rubbed Dalila's knee," Sudi said.

"And my thigh," Dalila said, her eyes huge. "I thought he was Carter's friend."

Sudi wrapped her arm around Dalila's shoulders. "The thought of getting caught making a move on you made it even more fun for Brian."

"He can't be trusted." Dalila shook her head and shuddered. "I never want to be alone with him, ever."

"I know that feeling," Sudi answered, and pulled a tube of gloss from her pocket. She opened it and spread tangerine color over her lips, then puckered and passed the gloss to Meri.

"Does he know anything about the cult?" Meri asked.

"We're still not sure," Sudi said. When Meri didn't apply the gloss, Sudi took the tube and put it on her lips for her. "But after we showered, we decided to come back here. We figured Abdel would have left the scrolls and—"

"—We wanted to find a spell to stop Apep from coming into our world." Dalila held her lips out for Sudi to shine. "There has to be an incantation—something. After all, the ancient Egyptians wrote the *Book of Overthrowing Apep*. It gives spells and instructions for stopping the monster; so why can't we find anything to help us?"

"That's why I came here," Meri said, but secretly she felt hurt that they hadn't called her. She looked at the scrolls spread across the floor. She couldn't believe that Sudi and Dalila had done that to the sacred text.

Dalila began rolling up a papyrus. "We thought we could find the answer," she said with a look of remorse, "but that's not an excuse to treat the Book of Thoth this way. I don't know what made me act so disrespectfully."

"Maybe trying to stop a giant snake that can swallow you whole requires extreme behavior," Sudi said. "We did the right thing."

Meri placed a comforting hand on Dalila's arm. "It's okay," she whispered.

But Dalila appeared truly ashamed. "I'm so sorry. I hope I didn't hurt anything. The hieroglyphs are so fragile." Her eyes were glassy with tears.

"It was mostly me, anyway," Sudi said, stepping forward to take the blame.

All three began to pick up the papyri and roll them. Meri dropped hers in a leather case and set it inside a trunk.

"So what did Brian tell you?" Meri asked.

"Just like always, he talked about how cool he is," Sudi answered, and then she sighed heavily. "If he did join the cult, and now I'm not sure that he has, I can't imagine the leaders entrusting him with any secrets anyway."

"He's exceptionally foolish," Dalila added, and then she collapsed on a stool. "What if we can't find the spell? What happens if we don't stop Apep?"

"Our next mentor will know what to do," Meri said, with a confidence she didn't feel.

A sound from downstairs made them stop.

The front door shut with a definite *clack*.

"Could the wind have done that?" Sudi asked.

"I closed the door," Meri whispered. "Someone just came inside." Her heart hammered. She hoped it was Abdel.

But then she heard the footsteps. A shuffling step was followed by a loud tap. After that came the shuffling noise again, of someone dragging a hard-soled shoe across the floor. Then another knock hit the floorboards, and immediately the shuffle sounded again. It didn't sound like Abdel's easy stride.

Meri looked at Sudi and Dalila.

"Do you think that's our new mentor?" Sudi asked.

Whoever it was started up the stairs, pounding heavily on each step. The old wood creaked under the visitor's weight.

"If that's our mentor, then the person is an old geezer," Meri said, trying to figure out the odd mix of sounds. "And whoever it is must weigh at least a thousand pounds."

"How are we going to get all of this cleaned up?" Dalila whispered frantically, panic in her face. Her fingers worked another papyrus, rolling it. "We can't let our new mentor see what we've done."

Sudi grabbed her hand. "We don't have time to pick everything up," she said.

"Then what are we going to do?" Dalila asked with a wild look in her eyes. "Should we transform?"

"I don't know about you two," Meri whispered, "but I'm definitely too tired. I'd get stuck in some in-between phase."

"We can't let our mentor find us," Dalila said. "How are we going to explain this?"

"We're not going to," Sudi said. "We'll hide, and after our mentor gets settled in for the night, we'll sneak out."

"Where are we going to hide?" Meri asked, looking at the stacked trunks and bookcases pressed against the walls.

"Here." Dalila slid beneath the table.

Sudi joined her. Then Meri squeezed between them.

The person had crossed the second-floor landing and was starting up the third flight of stairs. The harsh scraping sound made Meri cringe.

"We forgot to put out the light." Dalila gripped Meri's arm. "Our mentor will wonder why the oil lamp is burning."

"How are we ever going to kill a monster snake when we can't even handle something like this?" Meri muttered under her breath.

She scrambled across the floor to the shelf that held the oil lamp, then stood, licked her fingers, pinched the wick and put out the flame. The smell of smoke floated into the air.

As she started back to the table, a flashlight shone on Meri's face.

CHAPTER 16

Stanley Keene stood in the doorway, holding the flashlight in one hand and leaning heavily on Meri's wand with his other. His breathing made a harsh, annoying sound.

"Light the lamp again, Meri," he said, apparently not surprised to find her in Abdel's house. "Please, light them all."

Meri struck a match.

Stanley hobbled into the room, using the

wand as a cane. He stopped and gazed down at the scrolls still lying on the floor.

"Fascinating how these little drawings can be used to indicate sounds as well as the objects they depict." He tapped the tip of her wand on a hieroglyph that looked like an owl staring sideways at the reader. "That tiny creature represents an *m* sound."

"You know how to read Egyptian hieroglyphs?" Meri asked, lighting another wick and wondering why Stanley was there.

"Now," he whispered. "If only I'd known then."

She struck another match and watched him wander around the room, looking at the scrolls.

At last he found a papyrus, which had been tied with a string. A lump of mud covered the knot and was stamped with a seal. He picked it up and carried it back to the table. Then with a slow, strenuous effort, he sat on a stool.

He glanced down at Dalila and Sudi, still hiding under the table, and regarded them contemptuously.

"Cowering beneath the table," he said and frowned. "How do you expect to save the world?"

Sudi crawled out from under the table, and Dalila eased out after her.

His focus swung back to Meri, who was lighting the last line of lamps. Flames darted and curled, casting an orange glow about the room.

"Your wand doesn't work," Stanley complained. With a surge of wild anger, he beat the snake head against the floor. "It's supposed to ward off evil, and it didn't."

"I never said it would," Meri answered, bewildered, and stepped back to the table. She stood over him. "You *stole* the wand from me."

"Yes, my little cat," he said, calm again. His swollen fingers gathered her wet hair, then squeezed the ends and let go. Heat radiated from him, and she wondered if he had a fever.

"You knew the cat following you was me?" Meri asked.

"Of course," he answered. "I'm the one who sold the photos of you changing into a cat to the *National Enquirer*." He smiled in a way that made Meri wince. "One of my better assignments," he said.

"Why weren't you afraid of Apep?" Meri asked, trying to turn the conversation away from what he must have seen that night when she transformed.

"You could say I have special protection," he answered mysteriously.

"But why were you following me?" Meri asked.

"It's not just you." Stanley glanced around the table. "I've been watching the three of you since the day you were summoned, and now I've come to help you, before you destroy the world with your bumbling."

"You're our new mentor?" Sudi asked.

"We have so many questions," Dalila added eagerly.

"I said I've come to help you, not guide you," Stanley answered in a maliciously superior tone. "I pity anyone who is saddled with teaching the three of you the old ways," he sniffed.

"Then how will you help us?" Dalila said, adopting a tone and posture that made him blink.

"I know how to stop Apep," he said.

Meri sat down on the stool beside him. Dalila and Sudi drew closer.

"How do you know about Apep?" Sudi questioned.

"How do I know?" he whispered. For a moment, Meri thought he was going to cry. He sighed instead and rubbed his eyes.

"It started as an assignment," he said at last. "I had to cover the opening of the Anubis Spa. A fluff piece, I thought, but then I discovered, too late, that the cult leaders are a group of determined women and men who have used ancient rites in order to gain terrifying power."

"What do you mean, 'too late'?" Dalila asked, and rubbed his hand to comfort him.

"Because I didn't believe what I saw," he replied. "Who would believe that the ancient conflict between good and evil continues today? I doubted my own eyes. Is everyone so blind? And then, when I did believe, the cult had already cast its curses upon me."

He looked at Meri and sighed. "The three of

you are nothing compared to the powers they have, and yet the Hour priests have called on you to do the impossible. What kind of misguided faith must they have?"

"We'll learn what we need to know," Dalila said firmly.

"Perhaps," he answered. "I'll pray it's so."

"Tell us about Apep," Sudi interrupted. "You said you know how to stop Apep."

"The cult summoned Apep to destroy the three of you," he said.

"We know," Meri answered.

"The demon was small at first," Stanley continued, "and sent to kill you with its venom while you slept, but your cat Miwsher stopped it."

"Miwsher fought Apep," Meri said, remembering the storm, and how she had awakened to find a stray animal in her room.

"A lot of bad things happened that night," Stanley said, with unfathomable misery in his voice. "Apep has his own will, and the cult has lost control over the demon. Now only Seth can stop Apep. The three of you must summon the ancient god of chaos and storm."

"The cult worships Seth," Dalila put in, "so why don't they call him?"

Stanley frowned. "I'm surprised you don't know such a simple thing," he said. "Long ago, the goddess Isis cast a spell that still imprisons Seth in the chaos at the edge of creation. The god can't enter this world in physical form unless he is summoned by the divine pharaohs. You three are the only ones who can release him from that spell and call him into our world."

Meri looked at Dalila and Sudi, wondering if Stanley were telling them the truth.

"We'll never do that." Dalila folded her arms over her chest.

"To save the world from Apep," Stanley said, "you must."

"How do we know you're telling us the truth?" Sudi asked.

"We won't do it," Meri said firmly.

"If that is your decision," Stanley said, "then you alone will pay the consequences, and I've done my job."

He placed the scroll under his arm, shifted his weight, and, using the table edge as a brace, stood.

He started for the door, shuffling his feet, and tapped the wand on the floor.

Meri joined him at the top of the stairwell.

"Why did you visit my mother?" she asked. "You were with her the morning after the storm, and I heard you mention the Cult of Anubis when you got into the car with her."

"I thought your mother could help me," he said, starting down the steps. "Especially after I discovered the way she stole you out of Egypt."

Meri bristled at his choice of words. "She adopted me," she said, following him down the stairs.

"Hmph," he snorted, taking another step. "'Kidnapped' is a better word."

"What do you mean?" Meri asked.

Dalila and Sudi hurried down the steps so they could listen.

"I was the late-night visitor you were asking about that day after the storm," he explained as he started across the second-floor landing.

"You were the one who knocked on the door?" Meri asked. "Then that means you stayed until morning talking to my mother."

Stanley grinned. "When I mentioned the Cult of Anubis to her, she opened the door to make sure no one was outside listening."

"Why would my mother be so cautious if she truly believes the cult is no more than a silly fad?" Meri asked as they walked down the last flight of stairs.

"Precisely," he answered, stopping to catch his breath before he spoke again. "Why did she become so nervous? I assumed she knew something that could help me."

Sudi and Dalila joined Meri and put comforting arms around her.

"Did she?" Meri asked at last.

Stanley started to answer, then stopped and wheezed. He labored to pull in air. His cheeks turned from red to an odd purplish color.

"Maybe you should sit down on the steps," Dalila suggested. "You don't look very well."

He shook his head sharply and quickened his pace. "I've said too much," he whispered. "That's all."

By the time he reached the front door, he had a strange desperation in his eyes.

"Help me," he whispered as he fell on the stairs with a loud thump. He clutched the wand and papyrus tight against his chest.

Meri placed her hand on his forehead. The skin felt cold and wet.

He pushed her hand away.

"I think you're having a heart attack," Meri said.

"Don't you know anything?" he asked. "Can't you see what is happening to me? You're supposed to use the magic of the gods to protect the world, and yet you don't know?"

Sudi flipped open her cell phone. "I'll call an ambulance."

"Doctors can't help me." Stanley grabbed the phone from her and snapped it closed. "Since the beginning of time, the divine pharaoh has been charged with keeping the cosmic order and stopping the forces of chaos that threaten the world. As royal Descendants, you're failing."

Suddenly, Meri felt the presence of another force building around them, something cold and ancient and evil.

Stanley looked up, and his jagged breathing gave way to silence. His eyes widened as his arms and legs stretched and a guttural sound came from his throat.

Meri screamed and shielded her eyes.

When she looked again, Stanley had dissolved into a cloud of specks that fell like a powdering of dust on the floor.

Meri jumped back and batted the particles away from her, trying not to inhale them. She opened the door, stepped out onto the porch, and took a deep breath.

"Yuck," Sudi squealed and ducked, rushing toward the door. She joined Meri outside.

Dalila groped through the dust until she was outside, too; then she leaned over the porch railing, coughing and crying.

"How could he just disappear?" Meri asked, trying to blot out the image of Stanley vanishing.

"Even though we possess our own identity," Dalila explained, "the gods can still use us to deliver messages. I think Seth was trying to use Stanley, but when Stanley fought to tell us what we needed to know, Seth called him back."

"What did we need to know?" Meri asked. "That we're failing?"

"No," Dalila said. "Stanley managed to tell us that Isis had cast a spell imprisoning Seth. I doubt that Seth wanted Stanley to give us that information. And I think Stanley was trying to tell us more in spite of what was happening to him."

When the particles had settled over the floor and stairs, Meri stepped back inside, grit crackling under her feet, and picked up the scroll and the wand.

"I can't believe it," Sudi said. "Just like that, Stanley's gone."

Dalila bent down and touched the grains. "I think this was more a show, to frighten us and convince us of Seth's power. Stanley was probably transported to another location."

"I hope so," Meri said as she stepped outside again and rejoined Sudi and Dalila on the porch. "I hate to think that I was just walking over what's left of Stanley."

Sudi pointed to the seal on the papyrus. The hieroglyph for Seth, an erect tail and a pair of angular, raised ears, was imprinted on it. "Open it, and see what Stanley was trying to steal."

Meri broke the seal, untied the string, and unrolled the scroll. The papyrus felt heavier and the fibers rough, different from the ones she'd touched before. She winced, wondering if the magic within was more powerful because the spells were used to battle the lord of chaos.

"*Sexem a xesef a madret a,*" Dalila intoned, reading the first spell aloud. Then she translated: "I gain power over and repulse the evil which is against me."

"It looks like all the spells are ways to free oneself from Seth's control," Sudi said.

"Poor Stanley," Meri whispered. "He was probably stealing this so he could get out from under Seth's control."

"Maybe Seth is the only answer," Dalila said. "Wall paintings in tombs show him on the prow of the sun god's barge, fighting Apep."

"Seth stands for evil and destruction," Sudi reminded her. "He's too dangerous to call forth."

"We'll find the same incantation that Isis used to imprison Seth," Dalila said confidently. "Then, after Seth has destroyed Apep, we'll send him back to the chaos at the edge of the universe."

"Are you sure?" Meri asked. "If Seth was

controlling Stanley, then how can we trust anything that Stanley told us?"

"You're holding a scroll that proves that Seth can be overpowered," Sudi said.

"I know," Meri said, hating the way her fingers quivered.

"Tomorrow night," Dalila said firmly. "We'll meet at the Tidal Basin and summon the god."

"And if we do bring him here, will he really obey us and destroy Apep?" Meri asked.

"He's destroyed Apep before," Dalila answered.

"But so have we," Meri said, feeling doubtful. "It feels so risky. We could end up with both Apep and Seth loose in our world."

"The Book of Thoth gives us the power to command the ancient gods," Dalila argued.

"It hasn't helped us with Apep," Meri countered.

"That's the reason we need to summon Seth," Sudi added.

"All right," Meri said at last. "Tomorrow night." But she didn't feel convinced.

After a moment, Meri went back upstairs and

extinguished the lamps. Then, downhearted, she started home, carrying her wand, and the papyrus that Stanley had tried to steal. She wished she had the answers.

CHAPTER 17

Meri stepped into the front room. Her mother was sitting in the rocking chair near the fireplace. She didn't look like a future president of the United States, wrapped in her purple afghan. She looked vulnerable and small, and in the firelight Meri saw a mix of fear and sadness on her face.

Meri dropped the papyrus in the umbrella stand and set her wand against the wall; then she walked across the room.

Her mother turned.

"Have you been crying?" Meri asked as she stepped toward the hearth and kissed her mother's cheek.

"No, of course not," her mother said and sniffled. "Have you ever seen me cry?"

Meri shook her head. But then her mother's eyes brimmed with tears.

"What's happened?" Meri asked.

A jangling sound made Meri look down. A pile of red, green, and blue beads was cupped in her mother's hands. The semiprecious stones glinted in the firelight.

"I need to tell you the truth before it becomes headline news," her mother said. "Sit down."

Meri pulled a chair up next to her mother. She sat beside her and watched the fire. The embers pulsed within the pile of ash.

"I want to be president," her mother began softly. "You know that better than anyone, but it's another kind of power that has always interested me."

"What other?" Meri asked.

"The power of spells and incantations," her mother answered. "Does magic really exist?"

Meri held her breath, then blurted, "Why are you asking me?"

Her mother turned and took Meri's hand. "Because ten years ago, when I saw you on the streets in Cairo, I stepped into another realm, or at least I think I did. I'm certain not everything that happened that day was my imagination."

"I remember the afternoon," Meri whispered. She had been holding Miwsher and meandering through the crowds outside the Cairo museum. Tourists had given her money in exchange for having their picture taken with her.

"You need to know everything that happened," her mother went on, "so you'll understand why I did what I did. When I walked past you—maybe it was the glint of sun—I don't know, but I saw your birthmark, like a brilliant white light, beaming from you. I know I couldn't really have seen it, because your hair was thick and long, like it is now."

"You never told me this before," Meri countered. "You always said you saw my little face and fell in love with me."

Her mother looked away from her and stared

into the fire. The shadows on her face stuttered in the firelight and made her look old.

"You have an odd birthmark on your scalp," her mother said quietly. "It's the sacred eye of Horus. Do you know what that is?"

Meri nodded.

"If I hadn't seen the birthmark," her mother confessed, "I probably would have walked past you."

Meri looked down and blinked to keep the tears from her eyes.

"I'm sorry," her mother said. "I was with a delegation, and we didn't have time for such—"

She stopped, but Meri knew she had almost said, "nonsense."

"That day I crossed a threshold into a world of magic," her mother said, and gazed back into the fire. "As strange as it sounds, I sensed that evil forces were trying to kill both you and Miwsher. Maybe too much sun was giving me heatstroke. I don't know, but I decided to adopt you. And it was more than a decision. I felt as if my entire life had pushed me to that moment. I told the Egyptian officials who were with me that if you were an orphan, then I wanted to adopt you and take you home with me."

Her mother paused and wrapped the afghan more tightly around her shoulders and across her chest, even though the room was overheated.

"The translator asked you about your family," her mother stopped and laughed, not aloud, but to herself, in a sad tone that sent a shiver through Meri. "You told her that Miwsher was your mother."

Meri gasped. "Why haven't you told me this before?"

Her mother ignored her question and continued, "The officials loved your story and called you a child of royal blood. Then one of the government men told me the story about the cat goddess Bastet mothering the pharaohs. They thought you were delightful."

Meri had vague memories of her life in Cairo—the kindness of the neighborhood women, their warmth and love—but she had no memory of a home, a mother, or of Miwsher being more than her pet.

"It was a while before you spoke English, and even after you did, you insisted that Miwsher was your mother, that your cat turned into a woman."

"I don't remember saying that," Meri said, feeling her chest tighten. "I would remember something so strange."

"Sometimes at night, even now," her mother went on. "I hear prowling around the house— sounds only a human can make by opening the refrigerator or the sliding glass door, and when I investigate, I always find Miwsher alone."

As if the cat understood, she stretched and meowed, then sat and blinked at them.

"Yes," her mother said to Miwsher. "I find you staring up at me with that smug little feline smile that probably exists only in my imagination, but still, late at night, I've wondered if you really do transform into the goddess Bastet."

Then her mother laughed again, and her laughter sounded strange. "Can you imagine if the opposition party could hear me say that?" She shifted the beads to one hand, and a strand fell across her lap. That was the first Meri had noticed that the beads were strung together.

Her mother leaned closer. "I forged documents

and brought you both home with me," she whispered. "I broke the law."

Meri took in a deep breath. Her mother's reputation was impeccable. The opposition party was always trying to create a scandal or find something in her past, but without success. What would happen if they discovered her secret?

"By the time the plane landed in California, the magic was gone, and I couldn't believe what I had done," her mother went on, "but I adored you. I had never been as happy as I was when you were in my arms."

Her mother began rocking. The curved slats of the rocker creaked noisily.

"I don't believe it was a coincidence that brought us together that day," her mother said, staring up at the ceiling. "I think the universe was weaving our lives together, purposefully, and with a plan."

Meri felt a sudden urge to tell her mother the truth, but she held back. Her heartbeat quickened, and she waited to hear what else her mother had to say.

"Over the years, one lie built on another," her

mother said. "I was always amazed that no one found out, and then, somehow, Stanley Keene did."

"Did he tell you how?" Meri asked.

"No," she said. "He threatened to print the story unless I joined the Cult of Anubis. Why would he want me to do such a silly thing?"

The wood crackled, and flames shot up the chimney.

"Did you join the cult?" Meri asked, aware that her voice was trembling. She changed her position so her mother couldn't see the shaking in her knees, and wondered if Seth had been controlling Stanley even then. Or maybe Stanley had been hoping that if her mother saw the truth she'd use her position in the government to stop the cult.

"Of course not," her mother answered. "I think Stanley was having mental problems. His family has reported him missing. He hasn't been home since that night. And whoever heard of black-mailing someone into joining a spa? Ridiculous."

"I'm glad you didn't," Meri said in a weak voice.

"I won't be blackmailed, and I told him so," her mother said. "I don't care what it costs me, even if I lose my seat in the Senate. I only wanted you to hear the truth before the rest of the world knows."

Meri knew Stanley wasn't going to run the story, because he didn't exist anymore. Or, if he did, Seth had taken him someplace far away. At the same time she sensed that her mother wasn't telling her everything. After all, Stanley had spent half the night with her. They must have discussed something more.

Her mother leaned over and poured the beads into Meri's hands. "This is the necklace you were wearing the day I found you," she said.

Meri examined the large amulet attached to the strings of beads. "I don't remember it."

Her mother stood and dropped the afghan on the rocker.

"Why are you giving it to me now?" Meri asked.

"Because I sensed that you needed it now," her mother answered mysteriously.

"What did Stanley tell you that you're not saying?" Meri asked.

"I belong to the intelligence committee," her mother said. "I know that some things must be left unsaid, because to speak them could create more problems than already exist."

"You have to tell me," Meri pleaded, following her mother across the living room. "Mom, I have to know what Stanley told you."

"Why?" her mother looked back at her. "Should I believe the things he said?"

"You gave me the necklace," Meri replied, "so you must believe."

They stared at each other for a long moment.

"I love you, Meri," her mother said. "If something happened to you, what I would have left in my life wouldn't be enough."

"Mom, you're scaring me," Meri said, but her mother was already heading up the stairs. "Do you know who I am?"

"Yes," her mother answered. "You're my beautiful daughter."

CHAPTER 18

Night pressed against the windows, and the changing pictures on the six TV screens reflected off the glass, flashing and jumping as one story changed to the next. The sound was off.

Meri sat in her mother's chair, alone in the room, the necklace spread out on the table in front of her. She studied the hieroglyphs etched in the amulet. Her fingers began to tremble as she traced over the symbols.

"*Heka*," she whispered, reading out loud. "Divine magic."

"*Sia*." She read the second word aloud and translated it as well. "Divine knowledge."

And then she uttered the last word, "*Hu;* divine utterance."

She didn't understand why the words filled her with such hopelessness. Maybe it was because she didn't have the answers but knew she should. She turned the amulet over, hoping to find a clue on the back.

The words *medou netjer* were written there. The hieroglyphs meant "the words of the gods." But that didn't help her, either. She wondered what her mother knew, if anything, and why she hadn't told Meri more.

Carefully, she placed the necklace around her neck. A clasp was missing, or one of the lengths was broken, because she couldn't figure out how to wear it. She took it off again and wrapped the strands of beads around her arm, then placed the amulet in her palm and returned her gaze to the television sets.

The topic on channel seven changed to the weather.

Meri grabbed the remote and turned up the volume.

A commentator's voice filled the room.

She wished the noise would wake her mother. She didn't want to be alone, but her mother had a full schedule tomorrow, ending with a fund-raiser at the Willard Hotel, and she needed her sleep.

Meri sighed, disheartened, and stared at the TV.

Geologists, meteorologists, and volcanologists had come to D.C. to study the freak storms. Scientists agreed that the current temperature, moisture, wind velocity, and barometric pressure could not produce cumulus clouds, but as of yet, no one had a theory to explain what had.

The next segment showed silver weather balloons being released and floating into the clear turquoise sky near the Washington Monument.

Meri muted the sound from that program and turned up the volume on a second.

A reporter's voice boomed, "Tomorrow, geologists will send a probe under the earth's crust to see if magma is building and releasing gases that are affecting the local climate."

Meri pushed a red button and turned off that television.

Most stations were interviewing people who had gathered in front of the White House with signs. A family stood behind a handmade poster that proclaimed the end of the world. Other groups carried banners that blamed global warming for the freak storms. A few men and women held placards that said aliens from outer space were changing the atmosphere.

Meri was about to turn off all the sets, when the words *breaking news* flashed across the bottom of the last TV screen.

In the picture, a reporter stood in front of the Tidal Basin.

Meri turned up the volume and watched.

The reporter stepped next to the broken fence, then leaned over and ran her fingers through the slime that covered the walkway. She crinkled her nose, seeming to smell something disgusting. "Is this a Halloween hoax, or is there a monster loose in the District?" she asked, staring solemnly into the camera. "Tourists reported seeing a snake that was as long as a city bus."

Then the camera panned, and, under the harsh lights held by the TV crew, the reporter followed the trail of dead grass and mucous that led to the broken chain-link fence. She held a handkerchief over her nose and joined a group of tourists who didn't look very happy to be standing next to a splintered tree. Their eyes kept shifting in a watchful way, appearing terrified that the creature might return.

The reporter took the white piece of cloth away from her mouth and spoke to a lady whose sagging belly was covered with a long green T-shirt.

"Tell us what you saw," the reporter said.

"It looked like a giant slug," the woman answered, waving her hands, "and I think it bit that tree into pieces."

No sooner had she spoken than a man pushed in front of her.

"I sure hope the government hasn't been doing some weird biological research," he shouted, "because I saw something that doesn't belong in the natural world!"

Meri turned off the last set and sat in the dark, wishing she heard the soft steps of her mother coming into the room to comfort her. But the house remained silent. Slowly, she stood up and walked outside. She sat on the edge of the rock garden and looked up at the starry night. Staring into that vast dome of space, she felt as if she knew the secret of all secrets: the divine did exist. The universe wasn't an accident, and knowing that, the immensity of what she had to do overwhelmed her. What would happen if they couldn't stop Apep?

Abdel had said that Descendants who failed were sent to live in the chaos at the edge of creation. But, her fear wasn't for her own fate; she was afraid of what she and her friends were going to unleash on the world. They needed a solution, and she didn't think Seth was the right one.

"You've put too much on me," she whispered to the night sky and wiped at her tears. A breeze curled around her, bringing dampness from the Potomac River. Glistening drops of moisture settled on the lawn.

If Meri and her friends did summon Seth tomorrow night, she feared that they wouldn't be able to control the ancient god. What if releasing him from the old spell and allowing him to come back were the spark that started the end of the world?

"Help me," she prayed. Closing her eyes, she confessed, "I'm afraid."

A hand touched her shoulder.

She cried out and turned.

Miwsher sat on the stone ledge behind her, looking very much like an ordinary cat. Had Meri only imagined the touch, or had Miwsher tried to comfort her? She picked her cat up, petted the soft fur, and cradled Miwsher against her.

Miwsher nestled against Meri's neck and purred loudly, trying to console her.

CHAPTER 19

The birds began to twitter before the sky had even turned gray with morning light. And by the time the rising sun had tinted the tree branches pink, the smells of bacon and coffee were coming from the house. Meri had spent the night outside, trying to come up with a plan. She had none. That meant in twelve hours she and her two friends were going to summon an arcane god, the lord of chaos and storm, who had tried once before to destroy creation.

"Good morning," Meri said as she stepped inside the kitchen.

Georgie gave a startled jump and dropped her spatula. She bent to pick it up, then looked at Meri and stopped.

"Were you locked outside all night?" she asked, as she hurried around the kitchen island. "You look ill." She placed her warm hands on Meri's face and gasped. "You're as cold as death."

"I'm not going to school today," Meri replied and pulled away. "I need to sleep."

Georgie followed her into the living room. "Do you want me to bring you some breakfast?"

Meri shook her head and picked up the wand from the place near the door where she had left it the night before. "I think I might have a touch of flu," she lied as she took the papyrus from the umbrella stand. "I'm going to spend the day in bed so I won't miss the fund-raiser tonight."

"That's a good idea," Georgie said, but anxiety laced the old woman's voice, as if she sensed that something unthinkable had happened to Meri. She leaned against the newel post. "You'll call me if you need anything?"

"I'll call you." Meri continued up the stairs. She felt too tired to shower or even take off her sweats.

In her bedroom, she unwound the necklace from her arm. The beads clattered into a pile as she set them next to the papyrus on the nightstand. She prayed for guidance and hoped a plan would come to her in her dreams. Then she crawled into bed and snuggled under the covers, wanting nothing more than to have sleep take her.

She had just fallen asleep—or thought she had—when a familiar voice awakened her. "Your mom said you needed help getting ready for the fund-raiser."

Roxanne leaned over Meri, her flowery perfume filling Meri's lungs.

"I guess I can see why," Roxanne went on. "Did you sleep all day? What are we going to do about those swollen eyes? Everyone is going to think you've been crying."

"I can dress myself," Meri said, trying to tug the covers back over her head.

"Then why aren't you dressed?" Roxanne asked. "It's almost time to leave."

Meri sat up with a jolt, and they bumped heads.

"Ouch!" Roxanne jumped back and pressed her hand against her forehead.

"What time is it?" Meri asked, looking at the dark sky outside her window. She imagined Sudi and Dalila waiting for her at the Tidal Basin.

"It's almost seven," Roxanne said. "But I'll have you ready in time. Don't worry."

"Were there any storms today?" Meri asked as she threw back her covers and sprang out of bed.

"If we'd had one, it would have awakened you," Roxanne said. "That thunder is the worst I've ever heard."

Meri reached for her phone to see if she had any messages.

Roxanne grabbed it first and held it against her chest. "You have to get ready," she said. Then she set the phone down and handed Meri some lacy black underwear, still wrapped loosely in pink tissue. "Go shower," she ordered, "and put these on."

Meri locked herself in the bathroom and turned on the water. She stripped and grabbed a bottle of honeysuckle-scented soap, then doused it over her belly and scrubbed. She washed her hair, and then turned off the shower. After drying off, she put on the silk panties and the push-up bra and walked back into her room with the towel wrapped around her. She was still dripping wet.

Roxanne took the tail of the towel and patted at the soap bubbles sliding down Meri's arms. "I know I said to hurry, but we have enough time for you to dry off. I'll get you there on time. I promise."

Roxanne stepped back and proudly held up two slinky black dresses, different from the boxy clothes she had purchased that were hanging in the closet.

"When I saw your picture in that scandal rag—"

"Has everyone seen it?" Meri asked, feeling a blush rise.

"You have a gorgeous body, and obviously I misjudged your style," Roxanne said, taking a dress off its hanger. "All those clothes in your closet are for a whimpering, fearful, young girl. I'm taking them back and giving you a sassy style that fits more with who you are." She handed the dress to Meri.

Meri held it up and stared at the plunging neckline.

"What were you doing, anyway?" Roxanne asked. "The photo looks like you were jogging naked in the rain,"

"No," Meri answered emphatically. "I wasn't. Is that what everyone thinks?"

"Who cares what they think? It must have felt incredible. If I ever get gutsy enough I might try it myself." Roxanne tossed a flimsy jogging suit on the bed. "And just in case the press asks about your midnight run in the rain, your mom wants you to tell them that this is what you were wearing,"

Meri wondered why her mother hadn't mentioned the photos in the *National Enquirer* to her, the night before.

"Just say you didn't realize it was so see-through when it got wet." Roxanne smirked. "I love your style, and it's time you showed the world your true self."

"Okay," Meri said, wanting to hurry so

she could meet her friends. Suddenly, she saw something dark wiggling across the carpet.

A cobra lifted its head. The skin of its neck spread into a hood.

Meri let out a startled cry.

"What?" Roxanne asked, turning around.

Meri stopped her. "I'm just so excited about the dress," she lied.

"I thought you'd love it," Roxanne said. "It's going to make your waist look even smaller. You might as well flaunt what you've got. Everyone's seen what you have anyway, so it's not like you're showing off."

"Right," Meri said. She waited until the snake slid into her bathroom. Then she let the towel fall to the floor, and she slipped the dress over her head. She stared at her reflection, awestruck. The bodice revealed more than her bathing suit.

"Has my mother seen this dress?" she asked.

"You look lovely," Roxanne cooed. "Why wouldn't she approve?"

"I need an Alka-Seltzer." Meri dodged back into the bathroom, slammed the door, and leaned against it.

Dalila stood in the corner, transformed. Her brown eyes widened, and she shot a surprised look at Meri.

"You look stunning in that dress," she said. "Is your mom going to let you wear it?"

"I guess." Meri opened the medicine cabinet. She pulled out the box of Alka-Seltzer and a glass.

"Sudi and I were so worried," Dalila said in a rushed voice. She stopped Meri before she put the box away. "The transformation makes me sick," she explained. "My stomach is still spinning."

Dalila grabbed an extra glass and dropped two tablets into it. "Where have you been?" she asked as she turned off the faucet. "We needed to talk to you. You didn't answer your phone, and you weren't at school."

"I was sleeping," Meri said.

Roxanne knocked on the door. "We really need to get started on your makeup," she said. "Are you okay?"

"I'm fine," Meri replied, and then she whispered to Dalila, "How did you get in?"

"I slithered in," Dalila said with a smile. "No

one expects to see a snake climbing up the stairs."

"What did you need to tell me?" Meri asked, not sure she wanted to hear the answer. She sipped the drink, the fizzy bubbles tickling her lips.

"People with cameras are camped out at the Tidal Basin near the broken railing," Dalila said and chugged her drink. She placed her fingers over her mouth to cover a burp. "They're all waiting for Apep. They think D.C. has its own Loch Ness Monster, and a radio station has even started a contest to name it."

Roxanne pounded on the door again. "Meri, are you sure you're all right? I can hear you talking to yourself."

"I'm practicing a speech," Meri lied, saying the first thing that came into her mind. "It's a surprise for my mother. I want to tell everyone at the fund-raiser how much she means to me."

A long, heartfelt *aaahhhh* came from the other side of the door.

Meri shook her head. "I can't believe I said that," she whispered, and then she asked Dalila, "So what are we going to do?"

"We'll still meet at the Tidal Basin, but on the other side, near the Jefferson Memorial," Dalila said. "Be there by ten."

"I'll be there," Meri answered, feeling her chest tighten, because that also meant she was going to have to walk out of the fund-raiser in the middle of her mother's speech.

"Summoning Seth is the right thing to do," Dalila said, sensing Meri's hesitation. "The newspaper said nine more tourists disappeared."

"I know we're doing what's right," Meri agreed, even though intuitively she didn't feel that they were. "Do you have the incantations?"

"I found the papyrus," Dalila answered. "The spell for summoning Seth is really long. It will take at least twenty minutes to recite." She frowned. "I hope no curious bystanders get in the way."

Meri shrugged. "We'll do our best."

"I'll see you later," Dalila whispered. Then she began reciting the spell, to transform herself.

A magic glow spun around her, lighting the room. A flurry of sparks shot into the air, and Dalila began to shrink.

Someone tapped on the door.

"Just a sec, Roxanne, please," Meri said. "I'll be out in a moment."

The door opened, and Meri's mother peeked inside.

Meri sprang forward, trying to bar her mother from coming in.

"Mom, I can explain," Meri said, even though she couldn't think of a lie to account for the reason that Dalila was twirling in the middle of the bathroom.

Her mother switched on the light. "Roxanne told me."

"She did?" Meri blinked in the harsh glare. When she looked back, Dalila was gone. A black snake wiggled across the tiles and hid behind the clothes hamper.

"I didn't know the fund-raiser was upsetting you so much," her mother said. "And you shouldn't feel nervous."

"Nervous doesn't even begin to describe what I'm feeling," Meri answered.

"You look beautiful," her mother said. "Everyone will be staring at you."

"Yeah," Meri agreed, but she had a feeling

they'd all be looking at her neckline. "I'm all right, Mom, really. Just a little queasy. If I don't feel better I might have to leave the dinner early."

"Not before you give your speech," her mother said with a broad smile.

"My speech?"

"Roxanne told me," her mother went on. "She said it was a secret, but she knows how I hate surprises. Don't worry. This one I love. I'm so touched."

"I can't believe she told you," Meri said, feeling her heart flutter. "I can't give the speech now. It won't be a surprise."

"Of course you can." Her mother stepped toward the doorway. "I wouldn't miss what you have to say for the world."

Meri groaned. How was she going to have time to write a speech?

"What's wrong?" her mother asked.

Meri placed her hands over her stomach. "Just the flu, I think," she said and promised herself that after this night, if she survived, she wasn't going to tell another lie.

"You'll get used to the nerves," her mother

said. "Be down at the car in twenty minutes."

"My hair's still wet," Meri said. "Maybe I should just stay home and wait until next time."

Her mother laughed. "Wet hair is not a challenge to Roxanne." She left the bathroom.

"Great," Meri said glumly and watched Dalila, as a cobra, slink through the doorway.

Meri stepped back into her bedroom as Roxanne came into the room, holding a pair of spiky sling-back shoes. She almost stepped on Dalila, not noticing the creature squirming near her ankle.

Ten minutes later, Meri stared at her reflection in the mirror. Her hair was pulled back in a knot at the nape of her neck, and her chandelier earrings tickled her bare shoulders.

"The person in the mirror doesn't even look like me." Meri wished Abdel could see her smoky eyes and glossy cheeks. She looked like a true Sister of Isis, a goddess and queen of Egypt. Maybe Abdel would have loved her enough to stay if he had seen her this way.

"That's you, sweetie." Roxanne stepped toward the door. "I'll give you a moment to go over your speech. I can touch up your makeup in the car." She paused in the hallway. "I almost forgot. Good news. Your mom said we can hire a makeup artist next time."

"Goody," Meri said, trying to fake enthusiasm. She doubted there'd be a next time.

As soon as the door closed, Meri went to her nightstand, grabbed the papyrus, and examined it again. Abdel had told her that the ancient Egyptians had used marsh reeds to make the strong, thin paper. They had split the stalks, then laid them across one another and pounded them into thin sheets. But this papyrus felt thicker and heavier than the others had. She studied the edge, then slipped her fingernail in between the fibers and ran it down the length of the scroll. Carefully, she pulled the two sheets apart.

Beneath the first papyrus was another.

Her heart raced as she began reading. Stanley hadn't been trying to find a way to release himself from Seth's command. He had been trying to steal the magic that Meri stared at now, so that the girls would have had no option but to summon Seth.

According to the ancient writing, Apep had

escaped Duat once before, but that time, Isis had stopped him without any help from Seth. She had traveled down to the Netherworld and found Apep while the creature was still in his lair. Then she had spoken the demon's secret names and ordered the serpent to remain in the land of the dead and not bother the living.

"Meri," Roxanne called from downstairs.

"Coming," Meri yelled back. She rolled up the scroll, grabbed her purse, and stuffed the papyrus inside, but as she started to leave her room, Miwsher meowed, and the sound made Meri stop. The feline cry came out very clear; enfolded in the yowl, her cat had said, *wait*.

Meri turned slowly, expecting to see a woman standing behind her.

Instead, Miwsher jumped on top of the nightstand and batted at the necklace until it fell on the floor.

"I'll take it with me," Meri said, rushing back to grab the beads. She opened her purse and slipped the necklace inside. "But I don't know what good it will do me. Can't you tell me what I'm supposed to do?"

Miwsher stared up at her, and a purr rumbled in her throat.

"All right, then, keep your secrets," Meri said and tenderly touched the tip of Miwsher's nose.

As she hurried from the room, she was already forming a plan.

CHAPTER 20

Meri tensed as the sedan pulled up in front of the Willard Hotel. News reporters and photographers crowded the stairs and carpet under the awning. A valet opened the car door, and when Meri stepped out, the photographers jostled one another to get closer.

Meri felt hesitant and shy, suddenly self-conscious about her neckline.

A noisy burst of flashes blinded her. People

shouted at her, each question overlapping the last.

She stood disoriented, wondering how she was going to climb the steps in her spiky heels with the explosion of afterimages clouding her vision.

A gentle hand clasped her elbow.

"Step and step again," her mother said jovially, guiding her up the stairs. Then they were inside.

"You're magnificent," her mother spoke in a soft, tender voice. "You can handle anything."

"I wish," Meri answered, feeling restless about what she had to do in less than an hour.

Mrs. Autry, one of her mother's aides, greeted them. She was dressed in a black pantsuit and held a clipboard filled with ruffled pages.

"We've had a lot of cancellations," Mrs. Autry said as she led them down the spiraling staircase to the ballroom.

Two men quietly joined their entourage. Meri assumed they were Secret Service agents or privately hired bodyguards.

"With all the media coverage on the weather and that Halloween snake," Meri's mother said, "I'm grateful that anyone showed up."

Nerves twittered in Meri's stomach. She wished she could tell her mother about Apep. Maybe the military could get rid of the beast.

Just before the doorway, her mother paused. She took a deep breath and straightened her back, then walked into the ballroom with long, elegant, presidential strides.

People at the banquet tables stood and applauded.

Meri peeked into the room. The gathering didn't look small to her. The crowd greeting her mother would distract her for another ten minutes. That gave Meri the opportunity to sneak out through the rear entrance, on F Street. She doubted any photographers would be waiting there.

As she started up the stairs, she heard someone crying in the women's restroom. Meri couldn't ignore anyone who sounded that miserable. She crossed the short hallway and tapped on the door, then pushed inside.

A girl wearing a shimmering white dress stood in front of the mirror, her hands covering her face. The long blond extensions looked like Michelle's, and so did the three-inch high heels.

"Michelle? Are you all right?" Meri asked.

"That's a stupid question!" Michelle wailed. "Why would I be crying if I were okay?"

She turned around, and Meri gasped.

Bright orange blotches covered Michelle's face. Rust-colored slashes ran across her forehead, and now reddish-yellow spots on her chin were starting to swell.

"I wanted Daddy to be so proud of me," she said, turning back to the mirror. She swept more powder over her face with a fluffy brush. "I just used a little self-tanning lotion to enhance my color so I'd glow tonight."

"Maybe you mixed products that shouldn't be used together," Meri offered.

"I'm always careful," Michelle answered and sniffled. "After all, it's my face. How did this happen?" She groaned and didn't wait for an answer. "Daddy will be so angry. He said this dinner was going to be crowded with people who matter, and he wanted me to look spectacular."

"Why would your dad care how you look at a reception for my mom?" Meri asked.

"Don't you know?" Michelle spun around and

stared at Meri. "Your mom hired my dad to be the fund-raiser for her campaign."

Energy drained from Meri, leaving an unpleasant emptiness in her chest. Even if she survived this night, which she doubted she would, her life was going to be filled with still more of Michelle's taunts and snide remarks.

"Don't look so unhappy," Michelle said, appearing glad the news upset Meri.

"I think that's great," Meri said, with fake enthusiasm. She wasn't supposed to use magic for her own advantage, but if she did something nice for Michelle, maybe Michelle would be grateful and stop harassing her.

"You probably just need to use a little soap on your face," Meri said, determined to give magic a try.

"Since when do you know about glamour?" Michelle asked unpleasantly.

Meri ignored the taunt and grabbed a paper towel. She added a little soap and turned Michelle away from the mirror.

"Close your eyes," Meri ordered.

Michelle did.

Beautiful Isis, queen of magic, hear my words, Meri said to herself as she wiped the towel across Michelle's forehead and down her cheeks. *I entreat you, goddess of love and healing, let the blemishes leave this one here and end her weeping.*

Michelle's skin glistened and changed back to her normal color and glow.

"The soap worked like magic," Meri said and turned Michelle back around to face her reflection.

"Wow!" Michelle whispered. She started to say thank you but stopped and looked at Meri as if she were seeing her for the first time that night. A scowl replaced her smile. "That dress is too risqué for you, don't you think?"

Meri glanced down, self-conscious again.

"The décolletage." Michelle shook her head pensively. "You helped me, now I'll help you," she said, tossing her makeup bag into her purse. "Maybe one of the waitresses has a sweater you can borrow."

"Does it look that bad?" Meri asked.

"Trust me." Michelle raised an eyebrow. "You need to cover up."

Meri touched her chest. Maybe she had

exposed too much. "I was leaving anyway," she said, turning to go.

"You can't leave." Michelle clutched Meri's wrist. "What will people say if you do?"

"But I don't feel well," Meri lied and tried to pull away.

Michelle caught her hand and led her back to the ballroom as Scott came down the stairs. He brushed his curly hair back and stared at Meri with a naughty tease in his eyes that surprised her. When he kissed her cheek, his lips lingered before he pulled back.

"You look amazing." He glanced at her chest, then hurriedly looked back at her face. "I don't know what you've done, but you should keep doing it."

His fingers slipped down her arm, and she wondered if he was flirting with her.

"She didn't have anything to do with her look," Michelle said with a pout. "It was her stylist."

"You know about Roxanne?" Meri asked, surprised.

"Daddy told me," Michelle answered as she added more gloss to her lips.

Meri wondered if Michelle's father was going to tell Michelle everything he found out about Meri's private life. She sighed. She didn't need to worry about the future until she knew for sure if she would have one.

As Michelle and Scott headed in to the ballroom, Meri turned to dash up the stairs, and bumped into Mrs. Autry.

"The senator has been looking for you," Mrs. Autry scolded. "Where did you go?" She didn't wait for an answer but marched Meri back inside the ballroom to the table near the front where Michelle and Scott were already seated. The room was filled with the luxurious smells of expensive perfumes and the lush fragrance of warming rolls.

Meri took her place, wondering how she was going to excuse herself and leave. Her stomach felt jittery, and she sensed she was already late.

She took deep breaths to calm herself, then pulled the necklace from her purse and studied the amulet. The bright light glinted off the gold and illuminated an indentation that she hadn't seen before. She pressed it, and the amulet opened.

Inside, engraved on the flat surface, was a curling snake. The goddess Isis in her avian form stood over it.

A waiter used tongs to set a piece of bread on a plate in front of Meri. She hadn't eaten since the night before. She grabbed a knife, buttered the bread, and took a huge bite, loving the rich butter melting over her tongue. As she chewed, she translated the hieroglyphs to herself: *the goddess Isis, beloved of the great living sun disc, did imprison Apep, using these secret names of the demon.*

"I can't believe you don't know the difference between a fish knife and a butter knife," Michelle said, holding up the proper utensil and buttering a morsel of bread.

Meri glanced up, then returned her attention to the list. Each name had been carefully defaced so that the writing of the names would not give Apep power. But the markings still left the names legible. Meri felt suddenly optimistic; possessing Apep's secret names would give her the power to command the demon and make him stay in his lair.

"I don't want your mother to lose the election because you have bad table manners," Michelle went on. "And why do you have those dirty beads on the table?"

"Because I'm going to save the world," Meri answered and glanced around. Maybe she could just stand up and walk out. Everyone would think she was only going to the restroom until time passed and she didn't come back.

Michelle sniffed. "You could at least use your napkin."

"I'm tired of being nice, Michelle, and I don't have anything left to lose," Meri warned and closed the amulet.

"What is that supposed to mean?" Michelle asked.

Meri dropped the necklace back into her purse. "I have more important things on my mind tonight and—"

"Like what?" Michelle asked snidely. "How to get another nude photo of yourself printed in the paper so you can show off your body?"

Scott reached over and rubbed Meri's shoulder. "Ignore her," he said.

Meri pushed back her chair and started to walk away. Suddenly her mother's voice boomed over the microphone. "My daughter had been practicing a speech for tonight, and I can't wait to hear it. Meri, would you like to give it now?"

Meri dropped her purse back on the table and held her hands to her cheeks, trying to push back the cat whiskers that were already prickling under her skin. What was she was going to say?

But as she started toward the podium, thunder shook the room. The dull, heavy sound rumbled beneath Meri's feet.

Lights flickered, and voices rose in fear and wonder.

Meri paused. Either Dalila and Sudi were summoning Seth, or Apep was coming back into this world. Whatever it was, Meri needed to be with her friends.

An elderly man with a curved spine raised his hand and stood. His poise and authority took the attention away from Meri.

"Senator Stark," he said, in a loud clear voice, "everyone is saying that the military has a new war technology that allows them to control the weather. Are these freak storms the result?"

"I can guarantee you that this weather is not

something the Pentagon has created," her mother answered with confidence.

"But if the information is classified," the man said, "you wouldn't be able to tell us if these storms were machine-made."

"I assure you," her mother replied.

As the diners began talking about the weather, Meri hurried back to the table, grabbed her purse and started to leave.

"I can't believe you're sneaking out when your mother asked you to speak," Michelle said loudly. "My father is right. Your mother needs a daughter like me if she expects to win this campaign."

"Michelle, get off it," Scott said. "That's not true. Everyone loves Meri."

"I don't," Michelle replied.

Meri spun around. Abdel had told her that she could never use the magic in the Book of Thoth for her own advantage. She took a deep breath and spoke an incantation anyway, knowing that for the second time that night she was violating a cosmic law.

"In the name of Isis, queen of magic, I return all the evil wishes and unkind thoughts you have sent me," Meri said under her breath. Then she turned her invocation to Isis and murmured. "Goddess of many names, I entreat you. May the thoughts that Michelle sends to me find a magical path back to her."

Meri hadn't even finished her whispered spell when a waiter holding five plates of salad lost his balance. Leafy greens slid over Michelle as the plates clattered to the floor.

"You did that," Michelle screamed, picking endive off her nose. "I don't know how, but—"

"I didn't do it," Meri said. "That's what you wished for me. So be careful what you think."

Michelle picked up her glass and tossed the water at Meri, but the water magically curled back and splashed over Michelle's face. She screamed.

The ballroom became silent. Everyone turned and looked at Michelle.

She pointed at Meri and shouted, "She did this to me, because she's so jealous!"

Meri left the room and didn't look back.

$\mathcal{Q}$

Meri ran to the back entrance of the Willard Hotel and, ignoring the surprised looks on the security guards' faces, kicked off her shoes, swung her purse over her shoulder, and bolted outside. The night pulsed around her with a strange quiver, and she wondered if the sensation came from something other than her fear. She sprinted down the sidewalk, then cut across Fifteenth Street and headed toward the Mall.

The pungent odor of grilling onions filled her lungs as she raced past tourists who were waiting to buy hot dogs from a street vendor. They stood in her way, gawking and pointing up. At first, she assumed the president's helicopters were passing overhead, but when she didn't hear the familiar thump of the rotary blades, she glanced up, and her heart skipped a beat.

Black mist bled into the night sky, seeming to come from an opening beyond the stars. A vein curled over the moon, and the vapor continued toward earth. Instinctively Meri knew it was the primal darkness seeping from chaos, carrying Seth to Dalila and Sudi.

Time was against her. She only had minutes to find Dalila and Sudi and stop them before they finished the spell. Adrenaline surged inside her. She intensified her pace and ran wildly, her purse bumping against her back.

Her thighs burned as she pumped harder. The fire in her muscles spread to her lungs. She raced up the hill past the Washington Monument, then down again to the water. Her breath came in jagged bursts. All at once she caught a glimpse of her friends through the trees.

Dalila and Sudi stood on the bank of the Tidal Basin, dangerously close to the edge, staring down at a papyrus. An eerie, convulsing shadow encircled them, but no tree, post or building accounted for the dark patch of shade hovering over them.

"Dalila! Sudi!" Meri yelled as she followed the path through the twisted trunks of the cherry trees. Branches slapped against her face.

They didn't stop or look up, but continued to intone a spell, seemingly lost in a trance. They didn't even respond when she was close enough for them to hear her rasping breaths.

The shadow thickened and closed around them, in a tight sphere, seeming to sense Meri's approach.

Meri shot her hand through the dark circle and was surprised when the shadow bit back. Her skin scraped over something that felt like the pointed scales of a horny toad lizard. She pinched an edge of the papyrus and ripped it away.

Dalila gasped and staggered back, stumbling out of the shadow.

Sudi blinked, then squinched her eyes and

shook her head. She looked around, disoriented, and waved her hands, struggling to fan the darkness away.

The shadow squirmed and writhed, trying to shroud Sudi and Dalila again. Meri lunged forward and swept her hands through the black cloud. It wiggled up into the air, then caught a gust of wind and whipped away.

"What was that?" Sudi asked, looking stunned.

"I don't know," Meri answered. "It was surrounding you."

Dalila shuddered and brushed her hands over her forehead. "The spell that summons Seth has power of its own," she said. "It dominated my will and forced me to continue chanting the invocation even after I wanted to stop."

"That happened to me, too," Sudi said, her eyes widening. "But I didn't want to stop, because something deep inside me wanted to please the lord of chaos."

"I don't think it was the spell," Meri said and pointed up to the sky. "I think Seth had control over you from the moment you spoke the first word."

Near the moon, the black vapor was recoiling,

the thin tentacles turning in and slipping away from the world, back beyond the stars. The natural rhythms of the night took over, and a gentle autumn breeze replaced the abnormal quivering of the atmosphere.

"We never would have been able to command Seth," Sudi said.

"What did we almost do?" Dalila asked. "If we'd been successful in summoning him . . ." She stopped. Whatever she had envisioned was too horrible to say. Then she leaned against Meri. "I'm glad you came late and were able to stop us."

Meri started to roll up the papyrus, but Dalila plucked it from her hands and threw it into the water. The ancient writing dissolved, and the papyrus floated away, no more than a piece of trash.

"I can't believe you did that," Sudi said.

"It was the best thing to do," Dalila said confidently.

"So, what now?" Sudi asked.

"I want to show you the papyrus that was hidden under the one that Stanley tried to steal," Meri said, opening her purse.

She handed the scroll to Sudi and Dalila. They unrolled it and began reading.

"It gives us another way to stop Apep," Sudi said. "But where are we going to find his secret names?"

"I have them," Meri said. "At least, I think I do." She took the beads from her purse, opened the amulet, and showed them the list.

"A *menat* necklace," Dalila said. "Where did you get it?"

"My mother said I was wearing it when she found me," Meri explained. "But a clasp must be missing, because I can't figure out how to wear it."

"I'll show you." Dalila took the necklace and placed the shorter strands of beads across Meri's chest. Then she lifted the longer chain, with the amulet, over Meri's head and let it fall down her back. "The amulet hangs down your back as a counterbalance to the beads in front and gives you divine protection."

Meri could feel the talisman dangling behind her.

"Then, when you need its power," Dalila went on, "you reach back, grab the amulet, and pull it forward, surprising your enemy." Dalila threaded the amulet through the space between Meri's body and her arm, finally placing it in her palm. "The pharaohs used the *menat* as a counterbalance to the huge gold collars they wore. I wonder who gave this one to you," Dalila said. "It looks as if it was blessed by the goddess Bastet."

Meri thought of her cat, but, instead of saying anything, she shrugged.

Sudi handed the papyrus back.

"To work the spell, we have to find Apep while he's still in his lair," Sudi said. "How are we going to do that? The last time we went into the Netherworld, a pissed-off god flung us there."

Meri stepped to the water's edge and looked down. "We're going to swim."

"No way," Sudi said. Her expression grew solemn. "We'll drown before we find Apep's underwater tunnel."

"I'm certain the entire Tidal Basin is the entrance Apep uses to come into our world," Meri answered. "We can dive down anywhere, and we'll eventually break through to the other side and enter Duat."

"The Netherworld is reversed," Dalila added, seeming to agree. "Legend says that the damned walk upside down. If this is the entrance, then the bottom of the Tidal Basin will be the surface of a lake in their world."

Sudi didn't look convinced.

"When the cult cast a spell and called Apep here," Meri went on, "I doubt that they created a single tunnel for him to use, because after he adjusts to our world he'll be able to come here exactly as he exists in the Netherworld. You remember how immense he was the first time we saw him?"

Sudi was quiet for a long while. "It's risky," she said. "What if you're wrong, and we swim down and find only mud? Will we have enough air to swim back?"

"We can't summon Seth," Meri countered. "What else can we try?"

Sudi looked away. "I hate this," she said in a small voice.

"I know," Meri answered.

Lightning flared across the sky, its reflection flashing and flittering over the tide pool. The wind picked up, and the water churned. Whitecaps lashed back and forth.

"Apep's starting to come into our world," Dalila said. "We need to stop him before he leaves his lair."

"Let's go," Sudi said, not sounding happy about what they were about to do. She took off her boots, then peeled down her jeans and stepped out of them.

Meri stripped off her dress and started to jump in, holding the papyrus tight against her chest.

Dalila stopped her. "You can't take the scroll," Dalila warned. "It won't survive the water. You just saw what happened to the other one."

Meri bit her lip. "I didn't memorize the spells."

Dalila and Sudi snatched the papyrus from her, unrolled it, and began studying the hieroglyphs.

"I'll take the first incantation," Sudi said. "Dalila, you memorize the second."

"I've got the last one." Meri started repeating the words in her mind.

"We can read the names from the amulet together," Sudi added.

Meri tried to focus on her incantation, but Sudi was reading hers aloud, and Dalila's teeth were chattering so noisily she couldn't concentrate. She should have thought of this before.

Cumulus clouds continued building into towering heads. Lightning stroked the earth, and the water throbbed and pulsed, reflecting the strobing light. Thunder ricocheted across the night, and raindrops spattered the papyrus.

"We have to go." Dalila took off her jacket and let it fall on the sidewalk.

Reluctantly, Meri rolled up the papyrus and put it back inside her purse. She worried that she hadn't memorized all the words she needed.

Sudi splashed into the water. Meri started after her, but Dalila still held back.

"What's wrong?" Meri asked.

"I never learned how to swim," Dalila said.

"We'll jump in together." Meri held out her hand. "Don't be afraid. I'm a strong swimmer, and I can take you with me."

"I know you'll protect me," Dalila said bravely, but her eyes showed fear. She took off her long skirt and stepped over to the edge.

Meri clutched Dalila's wrist. Dalila screamed as they plunged into the Tidal Basin. Icy waters slapped against them, and Dalila started to panic.

"Grab on to my shoulders," Meri said.

Dalila shivered violently. Her fingers trembled as she held on to Meri.

Meri curled and dove, swimming steeply downward.

Sudi swam beside them, her cheeks round, full of air. Then darkness engulfed them, and they swam blind, continuing down.

Meri pushed her arms forward, then stroked back. Her ears began to ache from the pressure, and her chest became strained. If they didn't break through the water on the other side soon, then she had brought her friends to their deaths. They were too far below to return without another breath.

CHAPTER 22

Light filtered through the murky water, and bits of debris floated past Meri. She knew at once that the surface was near. Strength swelled inside her. She stretched her arms in front of her, swept her hands back, and burst upward into the air. She gasped and drew a huge breath, then quickly looked around, searching for danger.

When she saw none, she concentrated on filling her starved lungs.

Dalila popped up beside her. Greenish-black scum covered her face. She held on to Meri's shoulder as brackish water spewed from her mouth; she gagged and spit, then dunked her head, getting rid of the slime.

"We made it," Sudi said breathlessly, as she dog-paddled toward them. "But I don't think that's a reason to celebrate." She turned over and did a backstroke toward shore, each breath followed by a short, broken cough.

Meri swam after her, pulling Dalila with her.

Bones bobbed in the water, knocking against something that looked like chum. Meri wouldn't allow her mind to consider what else drifted past her.

They sat on the muddy bank and stared out at the cavern. The lake was black and dull, and didn't reflect the flames that burned up the sides of the cave walls. Foul-smelling smoke rose from the fires, twisting into the dense haze that wreathed the long, pointed stalactites.

"It looks so different from what I remember before," Sudi said miserably.

"When we went into Duat the last time, we passed through the gates," Dalila explained. "The sun barge and the blessed dead, as well as the damned, go that way. But this time we used an entrance that leads only to Apep's lair."

"My emotions are all wrong," Meri broke in, wondering why such profound unhappiness had come over her. "I should be afraid, but instead I feel homesick, like I've been abandoned."

"Something's missing," Sudi agreed and tapped her chest. "I feel lost."

"The condemned are denied the revivifying light of the sun god," Dalila explained. "God pervades the world above, and we don't notice the divine presence, because it's always around us. Here we feel the complete absence of God."

"It's horrible," Meri whispered, fearing that if they stayed too long they'd lose all hope and never be able to return home.

"Let's get this over with," Sudi said, standing. "I hate it here."

Meri stood up and started walking away from the water. Soft, sticky mud sucked at her feet and oozed between her toes. Sudi and Dalila slogged along beside her.

An eerie humming filled the air—a dirge of

human cries from far away that blended into one constant sound. The wails grew louder until the keening became unbearable.

"Where are all those voices coming from?" Sudi asked.

"The condemned," Dalila answered. "In the ancient texts it says that the songs of the condemned rise in the morning and in the night, in a never-ending plea to the sun god for mercy."

They stepped through a craggy opening in the rocks and stared out at a wasteland of stagnant pools and filth, crowded with hundreds of bone-thin people.

The cries turned into shrieks as the condemned became aware that Sudi, Dalila, and Meri stood among them. Skull-like heads turned, and hollow eyes watched them.

"Jeez," Sudi whispered. "I don't think I have the strength to walk past them."

"It's the only way to find Apep," Meri answered with grim determination, stepping over a cadaverous man who tried to clutch her ankle.

Fires spit through the soggy soil, exploding around them.

A wail of immeasurable pain made Meri cover her ears.

A man dragged himself through the flames toward her. His skin blistered and split, peeling back like blackened petals. But Meri couldn't feel any heat radiating from the blaze.

"Help me," the man gasped, as he lifted his bony hand. His charred fingernails clawed at the air, trying to grab Meri.

She started to help him, but Dalila yanked her back.

"Don't touch him," Dalila warned.

The man screamed his outrage.

"But he's stuck in the fire," Meri answered.

"You mustn't pity the condemned," Dalila countered. "They did something atrocious once and knowingly excluded themselves from eternity."

But Meri's sympathy didn't go away. "He's suffering; they all are."

"They want you to feel sorry for them so you'll help them escape," Dalila said. "Even now they don't repent."

"They seem remorseful," Meri said.

"They're trying to convince you that they are,

so they can manipulate you," Dalila answered sternly. "Don't let them touch you. They'll steal your body and use it to return to our world, and your soul will be left here for Apep."

"Then stay close to me," Meri said, shaking violently. She locked arms with Dalila and Sudi. They stepped forward, trying to ignore the pleading looks and skeletal hands grasping for them.

They had gone only a short distance when the moans became chaotic, the voices wild with fear. The condemned squirmed and writhed over each other, trying to get away.

"What happened?" Meri asked. As she spoke, a strange and frightening tension wrapped around her.

"Apep is near," Dalila warned.

From the distance came the sound of something swishing over the mud.

Adrenaline shot through Meri; a cold sweat prickled her skin. Her breath came in rapid draws as her muscles tightened.

Apep appeared from behind a stony hill and sloshed toward them, through filth and decay, his massive girth wiggling and looping, circling over and around itself.

"Start the spell," Dalila ordered.

Sudi stepped forward. Her arms and legs were trembling, but her voice was strong. She raised her hands and shouted, "Fiend of darkness, demon of the west, we have the power of the goddess Isis and her magic. We are her sisters, the Descendants, and we come to speak your secret names, that you must obey us."

Even though Sudi was the one invoking the spell, Meri could feel the energy from the words.

Apep drew back and glared at them, trying to entrance them with his gaze. When they didn't look into his eyes, he opened his mouth, exposing his fangs, and bellowed. His roar shook the cavern walls. Fire spilled from the rocky perches and rained over the girls.

Undaunted, Dalila stepped beside Sudi, raised her arms and yelled, "Our magic comes from the great Isis, she of many names, who gave us the Book of Thoth. We command you to remain in Duat and not venture up into the world of light."

The words materialized, shimmering and re-forming into a lance that shot through the air and encircled Apep with white energy. The giant snake recoiled, then thrashed and rolled, splattering mud, trying to get rid of the spell that was melting into his scales.

Sacred magic quivered through Meri as she opened the amulet. She held it up so that all three girls could read the hieroglyphs inside.

"We call out these secret names," Meri said, "so that the serpent, who feeds on the dead, must obey us."

Then together, Dalila, Meri, and Sudi read: "*Shat ebut. He te tebe te she. Art ebu haya.*"

"We demand that you remain forever bound to the underworld," Meri shouted, finishing the incantation.

Apep stopped. He cocked his head to one side, his tongue flickering, seeming to anticipate more.

"Something feels really wrong," Sudi whispered, taking a step backward and pulling Meri and Dalila with her.

"I sense it, too," Meri said as they continued backing up. "What did we forget to do?"

"I'm sure we said the right incantation," Dalila added. "I'm positive we did."

Apep inched forward, testing them. His tongue shot out and wagged, inches from Meri's face.

"Do you think the incantation worked?" Meri asked.

"I don't think we should worry about that now," Dalila said, "because if the incantation did work, then the entrance to Apep's lair is starting to close, and we need to hurry."

"Let's go," Sudi said. "I definitely don't want to get stuck here." She turned to leave and nudged Meri. "Come on."

Dalila took the lead, sloshing through the mud, but when Meri started to follow, a soft, swooshing sound made her glance back. She didn't like what she saw.

She whirled around, and her feet sank into the silt. "Why is Apep following us?"

Sudi and Dalila joined her, each clutching one of her arms.

"We didn't tell him that he had to stay in one place," Dalila offered, and as she spoke Apep threw his body forward, squirming toward them.

"What do we do now?" Meri asked.

"Run!" Sudi yelled.

Meri tugged her feet out of the mud and tromped forward. "I think I forgot to add one little part when we cast the spell," she called out.

"What?" Dalila shouted, running clumsily. Grime splashed over her legs.

"I forgot to command Apep to allow us to leave the Netherworld without harm," Meri answered as she darted around a fire.

"It's not like we had time to memorize the spell," Sudi complained. She leapt over a woman sitting in her path. "We probably all messed up the words."

"It doesn't matter," Dalila answered, panting and gasping for air. "We'll outrun Apep. He'll never catch us."

Meri ran with her head down, her arms pumping at her sides. She felt grateful that her friends didn't blame her, but she also knew that she was the one who had forgotten to say the words that would have ensured their safety.

"Be careful!" Dalila shouted.

Meri looked up.

The condemned had crawled from their

hiding places and were crowding the path back to the lake. They squeezed against one another, weeping and howling, their hands reaching for Sudi, Meri, and Dalila.

"They want to use us to return to the world above," Dalila warned.

Meri hurdled over an outstretched hand. When she landed, she skidded in the mud and almost fell. Sudi caught her, and with a burst of energy, half dragged, half carried Meri forward.

Apep whipped over the thin bodies of the condemned, relentless in his chase.

The girls held hands and raced away.

By the time they reached the water's edge, Meri could feel Apep behind her, his fetid breath surrounding her.

"We can't fight him in the water," Dalila said. "He's too strong there."

"He'd swallow us whole," Sudi agreed. "Let's cast the spell again."

But already bubbles and waves agitated the surface of the lake. Something turbulent was rocking the depths below.

"There isn't time." Meri shoved Sudi into the

water. Before Dalila could turn, Meri pushed her hard, and she tumbled in with a huge splash after Sudi.

Sudi grabbed Dalila, and they stared up at Meri, surprised.

"I'm the one who forgot the words," Meri explained. "Leave while you still can."

"We're not going to go back without you." Sudi treaded water, holding Dalila.

"You have to," Meri said, hopelessly. "Don't let my death be for nothing."

Reluctantly, Meri turned and faced Apep.

The monster coiled around her, ravenous, eager for her soul. His breath, a bitter, venomous cloud, misted over her. She breathed in, and her lungs froze. Why had she believed she could possibly command the ancient gods and fight demons? Abdel was wrong. She was nothing: a nameless orphan from the streets of Cairo.

CHAPTER 23

T hrough her stupor, Meri became aware of a sharp twinge in her temple. Her birthmark throbbed, awakening her, forcing her to rise and stand. The soul of ancient Egypt pulsed within her—the power of the ages. Her chest heaved. She wiggled the numbness from her fingers, then reached behind her back and grabbed the amulet. As she brought the charm forward, her pain gave way to courage.

With her remaining strength, she jabbed the talisman into Apep's side.

The monster shrieked, releasing her from his deadly coils.

"I am a Descendant, a Sister of Isis," Meri said, her lips still sluggish, the words jumbled and slurred. "I command that you allow us to leave the Netherworld."

She pulled back her amulet and opened it, then recited Apep's secret names: *"Shat ebut. He te tebe te she. Art ebu haya."*

Apep recoiled. His tongue twitched irritably.

Meri stepped away, her feet numb, her thoughts groggy. This time, the demon had to let her leave. But when she reached the embankment, Apep's head shot around, and the tip of one fang stabbed her shoulder. Poison stung her and streamed under her skin, down into muscle and bone.

She cried out and fell to her knees, bending over in anguish.

Apep drew back, screeching his victory, his giant tail switching jubilantly as he curled over and around his massive body, sweeping away from her.

Meri groaned. She had failed again. She had

forgotten to add "without harm" to her command, and that mistake had left her without magical protection.

She dragged herself to the edge of the bank and rolled off, splashing into the water near Dalila and Sudi. The cold hit her chest and stole what little breath she still had.

"We'll help you," Sudi said, and tried to take her hand.

But Meri shook her head. "I'm all right," Meri lied. "You take Dalila back. I can make it on my own."

She filled her lungs and dove below the surface. She'd only slow her friends down, and she wanted them to survive, even if she couldn't. She extended her arms, ignoring the pain, and swam into the black depths.

Sand and pebbles roiled around her as the entrance to Apep's lair closed. Currents lashed back and forth, tumbling her about, and then the waters calmed. The barrier between the two worlds was again solid and secure.

Meri rose to the surface and floated on her back to the edge of the Tidal Basin, breathing in the aroma of an autumn night. The skies were clearing, the moon shining through the thinning clouds.

Sudi and Dalila pulled her from the water and helped her lie down on the walkway.

"You don't look very good," Sudi said. "I'm going to find help." She started to stand, but Meri grabbed her wrist.

"No one will know how to treat Apep's venom," Meri whispered. "Stay with me. I don't want to—"

Dalila pressed her fingers over Meri's lips before Meri could say, "die alone."

"Don't say it," Dalila pleaded, and began mumbling prayers.

Sudi wept quietly, her warm tears falling onto Meri's face.

Meri grasped her amulet as blackness clouded around her. She held the talisman against her motionless chest.

"*Medou netjer,*" she whispered to herself. She had spoken the words of the gods to save the world, and now she needed their divine help. She wanted to live.

"*Heka. Sia. Hu.*" She repeated the words inscribed on the amulet, calling forth the benevolence of the universe to let her stay.

The night became windless, the world still, and Meri started to rise out of her body.

A woman walked through the silence toward her and held up her hand.

"It is I, the great Isis, speaker of spells, divine protector of the Descendants," the woman said. "I come to you as mistress of charms and enchantments, to remove the serpent's venom."

She touched Meri's shoulder, placing her hand over the snakebite. "I have made the poison fall out on to the ground. You shall live, and the poison shall die."

Meri fell back into her body and sucked in air. She let it out with a jagged cough. Her lungs began working. Air wheezed in and out. A fire burned inside her, but she welcomed the pain; she knew it was life, coming back to her.

She blinked and the night became filled with noise again: the rumble of traffic and planes, and the excited voices of photographers camped on the other side of the Tidal Basin.

Dalila screamed with joy. "You're back!" she yelled. "I prayed we wouldn't lose you."

Sudi grabbed Meri and planted big kisses all over her face.

"Quit with the mushy stuff. You're suffocating me."

"How did you return to us?" Dalila asked as she helped Meri stand up.

"Isis was here," Meri said, feeling dizzy. She craned her neck to get a look at her shoulder. "She healed me."

"You have a mark," Sudi said, "but the wound is gone. It doesn't look like a snakebite, it—"

"Cool tattoo," someone behind them said.

All three girls froze.

Meri became suddenly aware that she was standing outside in wet, clinging underwear.

"Brian?" Sudi shouted.

Meri picked up her dress and yanked it over her head.

"Brian, why are you here?" Sudi demanded as she struggled into her jeans. A blank look crossed Brian's face. He shrugged. Then he glanced at the photographers across the lake. They had gathered their equipment and were racing down the walk-way toward Meri, Sudi, and Dalila.

"I came here to save your butts," Brian said gruffly. "Just get in the car."

He turned and started walking back to the giant Cadillac that was parked illegally on the grass, belching smoke.

"How did he drive his car into the park without getting caught?" Sudi asked as she picked up her boots. "I can't even toss a banana peel without having a dozen cops telling me to pick it up."

"Right now, I don't even care," Meri said. She grabbed her purse and started after Brian. "I just want to get away from here."

"Brian, did you join the cult?" Sudi asked.

"Hell, no," he said as he squeezed in behind the steering wheel. "You know I hate that touchy-feely junk."

"I think there's something magical about Brian," Dalila said, zipping up her skirt.

"Brian?" Sudi and Meri exclaimed in unison.

"Isis is using him," Dalila explained. "I'm certain that she is. The same way Seth used Stanley.

The goddess has provided us with a chauffeur and a ride home."

"Isis might be the goddess of many names," Sudi said. "But she's definitely got bad taste in boyfriends."

They crawled into the back seat of the Cadillac, and before Meri had even closed the door, Brian sped away.

Sirens sounded in the distance, but Meri was more concerned about the photographers who stood in their path.

Brian jerked the steering wheel to the left, and the car jounced wildly. The back wheels spun chunks of mud and grass into the air, hitting the photographers who were chasing after them.

Meri sank low in her seat and tried to hide her face.

"I'm going to be in so much trouble!" Sudi squealed. She bowed her head. "I'll be grounded until I'm twenty-one."

"The hell you will," Brian shouted, speeding through a red light. "No one's going to catch us. I borrowed the license plates from a black sedan parked by the FBI building before I did this deal." He grinned, proud of his cunning.

Dalila smiled, enjoying the reckless ride. "Isis knew that Brian wouldn't falter. Of all the young men we know—"

"—He's the biggest fool," Sudi finished for her.

"The one with the criminal mind, you mean," Meri said, praying no one ever found out about this night.

"But he is doing exactly what is needed to protect our secret," Dalila countered, with a satisfied look.

The tires squealed as Brian drove the car around the corner, and again at the next intersection. Meri glanced out the back window. The street was empty.

Finally, Sudi leaned forward. "Brian, no one is chasing us. Can you just take us home?"

Meri turned back in time to catch Brian's reflection in the rearview mirror. He looked disappointed.

"Yeah, sure," he said. The car slowed.

"Drop me off in Georgetown," Meri said.

"Why are you going back to Abdel's house?" Sudi asked.

"I'm not ready to face my mom yet," Meri explained.

Moments later, Meri was at Abdel's front door. She stole inside and climbed the stairs to the second-floor bedroom. She sat on Abdel's bed, then snuggled down into his pillows and breathed in the scent of his cologne.

As she started to fall asleep, the front door opened downstairs. She sat up in alarm, her heart beating frantically. She had been foolish to think that Seth would allow her to survive. The lord of chaos would demand revenge, and he undoubtedly knew that she was alone in Abdel's house, unprotected and vulnerable. A chill raced through her as she wondered who the ancient god had sent to destroy her.

CHAPTER 24

Meri crept across the carpet, her amulet clutched in her fist. She hid in the shadows at the top of the stairs and then slowly leaned over the banister, peering down into the room below. Abdel stood near the hearth, staring at the fire. Flames sputtered and sparked, and the faint smell of smoke filled the air.

"Abdel!" Meri cried as she ran down the steps.

He spun around, startled. "Meri, what are you doing here?"

She fell against him, loving the feel of his body. "I'm so glad you didn't leave after all." She hugged him harder. "I have so much to tell you."

"What happened?" he asked, still looking stunned. He touched the ends of her wet hair.

"You'll be so proud of what we've done," she said excitedly and began telling him everything, starting with the letter she had found in his jacket pocket.

When she had finished, he placed his hands on her shoulders and looked at her with something close to misery in his eyes. "The three of you promised me that you wouldn't act on your own," he reminded her. "What you did was dangerous."

"People were dying," she explained. "How could we wait?"

He shook his head. "Even the smallest ritual, when done without thought, can have unexpected consequences," he said. "Dalila and Sudi started to summon Seth, but then you stopped them before the spell was complete. The three of you failed to offer a counterspell to close the magic that Sudi and

Dalila opened. What will be the final outcome from that breach? You could have altered the very structure of the universe."

"We thought we were doing the right thing," Meri said, looking down.

"Meri, you were the reason I became an Hour priest," he confided.

"Me?" she asked. "How can that be?"

"You haven't lived those memories yet," he answered. "I never thought I would see you again, and now that I have . . ."

He didn't finish his sentence but instead kissed her with such tenderness and longing that she knew he thought this would be their last embrace. She closed her eyes and let her hands move up his sides. He gently pushed her back, before she was ready to end the kiss. She leaned forward for another.

"I can't let my feelings for you interfere with what I've been sent to do," he said. "I will fulfill my sacred vow to Isis."

"Isis doesn't care," Meri insisted. "She's the goddess of love, among other things. I know it's allowed."

"It's impossible," he answered.

"Nothing's impossible for me," she said adamantly. "I stopped the lord of chaos from coming into the world, and I battled the ancient demon Apep. I almost died tonight. I deserve more from you."

Then she realized what she had said, and she rushed outside, feeling foolish. Abdel came out onto his porch and joined her. His hands slipped around her waist, and he pulled her to him. He kissed her again.

That was what she loved about D.C.; the possibilities were endless. Magic happened here.

"Go home, Meri," Abdel whispered. He kissed her gently once more; then he went back inside.

She stepped into the shadows and changed herself into a cat, then stretched, enjoying the luxurious pulse of ancient Egypt that rushed through her. She didn't care what her mother, or Michelle, or Abdel thought. She had done the right thing, and had been true to her real self, a divine Descendant, an Egyptian goddess who had repelled the dark forces of chaos and saved the world. For a night.

DON'T MISS
THE NEXT BOOK

SISTERS
of
ISIS

3

Enchantress

Dalila feared she had made a terrible mistake. The worry kept nagging at her until she couldn't concentrate on anything her tutor, Mrs. Lavendish, was saying about the National Gallery of Art's exhibit on Netherlandish diptychs.

"Are you feeling ill, Dalila?" Mrs. Lavendish placed her hand on Dalila's forehead. When she lifted her arm, her blazer opened, exposing the gun in the holster cradled under her shoulder.

Dalila had recently learned that all of her tutors

had actually been bodyguards, ex-FBI types hired by her uncle to protect her from the people who wanted to kill her.

Mrs. Lavendish frowned. "You're trembling."

"I forgot to eat breakfast," Dalila lied, suddenly seeing her chance to run away. The plan was risky, but she had to find out if she had done something unforgivable.

"We'll get a snack in the café," Mrs. Lavendish said in her most soothing voice.

Dalila hated to lie again, but she did. "Let me use the restroom first. I'll be right back."

"Alone?" Mrs. Lavendish looked puzzled. Dalila had never tried to go off by herself before. Someone always waited by the door for her.

"You stay and look at the…" Dalila had already forgotten what the tiny paintings were called.

Mrs. Lavendish adjusted her blazer. "I'll go with you."

"I won't be gone but a minute," Dalila answered peevishly. She couldn't tell Mrs. Lavendish the real reason she needed to be alone. But her rude tone stunned Mrs. Lavendish enough to give Dalila the seconds she needed. She walked quickly away, though not so fast that Mrs. Lavendish would become alarmed and follow her.

When Dalila reached the rotunda, she darted into the checkroom. The attendant glanced at Dalila's number, then handed her a long rod inlaid with blue and green stones that mimicked the pattern of a snake's skin.

"I'm glad you came and got that thing." The attendant dropped it on the counter with a loud clank. "I swear I heard it hissing. What is it, anyway?"

"It's my magic wand," Dalila answered. Sometimes it was easier to tell the truth, especially when no one would believe you. She picked up the wand and nervously moved her fingers over the Egyptian hieroglyphs etched into the metal.

She left the museum and bounded down the front steps, then ducked and hid among the throng of tourists moving slowly toward the natural history museum. She had seldom been allowed out by herself, but after learning the truth about the meaning of her birthmark, she had become determined not to live such a sheltered life. After all, if she had to fight demons, then she should at least be allowed to go to parties and date.

A group of students in school uniforms crowded in front of her. They yelled and teased one another. Their antics reminded Dalila of how much she had missed. She had been homeschooled, and her only companions had been adults. She had never had a playmate or friend her own age until recently.

She followed the young students across the Mall to the carousel, then leaned against the fence, listening to the mechanical bells and their jarring melody. Mothers and fathers held their small children on the circling horses. Their smiles and laughter opened a deep sadness inside Dalila.

Her own parents had been killed in a cave-in while excavating a tomb in Egypt's Valley of the Kings when she was seven years old. Since that time she had lived with her uncle, the famous Egyptologist Anwar Serenptah. She loved him, but she needed her mother, especially now that she had so many questions about boys; well, not boys, exactly—just one, named Carter. Was it normal to feel so breathless when he put his arm around her? She thought of Carter, imagining the softness of his white-blond hair brushing across her face when he leaned down to kiss her.

A breeze caressed her. Though it was no more than a whisper of air, it pulled her away from her thoughts and made her wonder if it had been more than just wind. She had a growing sense that someone was watching her. Cautiously, she stepped back onto the pebble-covered path. Yellow leaves fell from the branches overhead and fluttered over her. She glanced around, wondering if Mrs. Lavendish had followed her after all, but she didn't see her, nor anyone else who could explain the tingling in her back.

People passed her and stared at her wand. Perhaps their curious glances were causing the uncomfortable feeling. Mrs. Lavendish had said the wand looked like the ornamental scepter carried by rulers on ceremonial occasions as a symbol of their sovereignty. That was close to the truth. The wand was supposed to be a symbol of her power as a magician, although she had no idea how to use it yet.

For some reason, her mentor, Abdel, had been holding back, not telling her everything she needed to know. Most of the knowledge she had had come from her uncle, who had taught her the old ways. Maybe Abdel didn't think she was smart enough to learn the sacred knowledge. She hadn't really mastered the one power he had given her: the ability to transform.

Dalila shuddered just thinking about it. She detested snakes. She had always been afraid of them, and now she became one: a fire-breathing cobra.

She sighed, straightened her back, and began hiking toward the Washington Monument. She had always thought that she had lived a sheltered life because she was being reared to marry a Middle Eastern prince. After all, she had royal blood. She knew that her family was descended from the ancient Egyptian pharaohs, but Abdel had told her the true meaning of her birthmark: she was a Descendant, destined to stand against evil and defend the world. She still couldn't believe that her uncle hadn't told her the truth.

She increased her pace and tromped forward, holding her wand like a shepherd's staff, tapping it hard on the ground. She repeated the words that Abdel had spoken over her to awaken the soul of Egypt lying dormant within her: "Sublime of magic, your heart is pure. To you I send the power of the ages. Divine one, come into being."

Just saying the words made her nerves thrum the way they had that night. Abdel had told her that back in ancient times, the goddess Isis had given the Hour priests the Book of Thoth and instructed them to watch the night skies. When the stars warned of danger, the priests were supposed to give the book to the pharaoh, so that he could use its magic to protect the world.

Nowadays, the Hour priests met as a secret society. When they learned that the Cult of Anubis had moved to Washington, D.C., they sent Abdel to find the Descendants born with the sacred birthmark. Only the divine heirs had the power to use the magic in the Book of Thoth. Dalila hoped that that was true, because so far, she and the two girls, Sudi and Meri, who had been summoned with her, hadn't done a very good job.

Their task was made more difficult by the fact that residents in the District believed the cult was a new age group from California. Authorities would never believe the truth: that the cult leaders worshipped the evil god Seth and used Anubis and the Book of Gates in unholy ways, to call forth demons and resurrect the dead. More than likely, if Dalila did go to the police, she'd end up with a court-ordered visit to a psychiatrist.

She crossed Fourteenth Street, her nervousness growing, as she followed the trail between the tall pine trees. Soon she was passing the Bureau of Engraving and Printing. To her right, the Tidal Basin glimmered in the late afternoon sun. She had a sudden vision of a hellish monster rising from the water and pulling her back under with it.

Some weeks before, she had tossed a papyrus containing a powerful spell into the water. The hieroglyphs had dissolved, but had the magic? Ancient Egyptians had viewed magic, *heka*, as the energy of creation, a power unto itself, and that had provoked her worries. If she had freed something evil, then she had to find a way to capture it before the cult found out what she had done.

She dreaded telling Abdel. She knew she should have been more cautious, but at the time she had wanted only to destroy the incantation. Her motives were right, but unfortunately the outcome could be disastrous. She took in a deep breath, fighting her uneasiness, and headed down to the Tidal Basin.

When she was certain no one was watching her, she leaned over the railing and stirred the water with the tip of her wand. Ripples spread over the surface in lazy waves, but nothing more happened. The tension that had been building in her muscles gave way, and she began to relax. She had expected the hieroglyphs on the wand to move, but they lay still beneath her fingers. Maybe her worries had been for nothing after all.

An unexpected rush of wind hit her, startling her. She cried out and almost dropped her wand. She caught it and fumbled with it, trying to hold on. The wand clanked noisily against the railing as she pulled it back to safety.

Finally she had it firmly in her hands, but she didn't understand why the blast of wind had frightened her so. Her heart was still hammering, and she had an overwhelming feeling that something bad was going to happen. She winced just imagining what would have happened if she had dropped the wand in the water. How could she ever have explained that to Abdel?

When she looked up again, an ugly, stout man stood near her. A scraggly tuft of hair grew from his chin, although the rest of his face was clean-shaven. His eyebrows met at the bridge of his nose, and in the light his eyes looked curiously orange, the black pupils rectangular instead of round. He blinked, and she realized it must have been the reflection of morning sunlight that had caused the illusion: his eyes were deep green.

Still, his abrupt appearance confused her. Surely she would have noticed him joining her, or heard him scuffling through the dead leaves that covered the walkway. She gave him a tentative smile.

The man glared in response.

She turned away, self-conscious, and plucked at her hair. Maybe he was staring at the birthmark near her temple. The sacred eye of Horus identified her as a Descendant but also marked her for death. Since she had learned the truth, she tried to keep it hidden, but maybe the wind had blown back her hair and uncovered it.

"I know who you are already." The man's words tore through her.

She glanced back at him and saw no friendliness in his gaze.